COOPER'S CORNER CHRONICLE

Cooper's Co... ...Snow Report

The ski hills a... and local busine... bustling as visito... to the Berkshires ... annual school ... Weather reports predict more snow, so every-one's in for a final round of wintry fun.

Lori and Burt Tubb of Tubb's Café say their restaurant has been busier than usual, and they're actually hiring more help. Philo and Phyllis Cooper report an increase in sales at the general store with the extra tourists passing through, and Clint Cooper says that Twin Oaks B & B is booked solid for the week.

"Visitors will find lots to do at this time of year," Clint reminds us. "Besides skiing and hiking, the museum in town has displays from

...featuring local artisans." The last word about things to do this week goes to Father Gallagher of St Bridget's parish. "For those in need of the luck of the Irish, the annual St Patrick's Day dinner and dance will take place Friday night at St Bridget's. Visitors to our lovely town are especially welcome!"

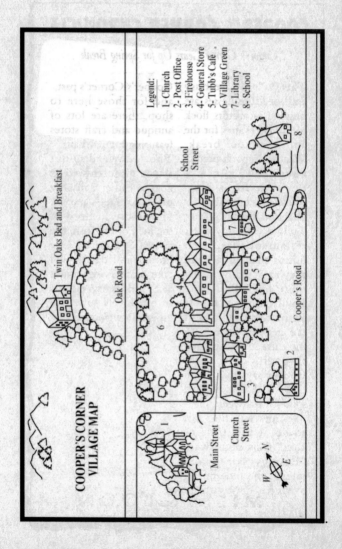

COOPER'S CORNER
VILLAGE MAP

Twin Oaks Bed and Breakfast

Oak Road

Main Street

Church Street

Cooper's Road

School Street

Legend:
1- Church
2- Post Office
3- Firehouse
4- General Store
5- Tubb's Café
6- Village Green
7- Library
8- School

COOPER'S CORNER

MURIEL JENSEN

For the Love of Mike!

MILLS & BOON®

*MILLS & BOON and MILLS & BOON with the Rose Device
are registered trademarks of the publisher.*

*First published in Great Britain 2005
by Harlequin Mills & Boon Limited,
Eton House, 18-24 Paradise Road, Richmond, Surrey TW9 1SR*

© Harlequin Books S.A. 2002

Muriel Jensen is acknowledged as the author of this work.

ISBN 0 263 84694 6

142-0805

*Printed and bound in Spain
by Litografía Rosés S.A., Barcelona*

To the Dinner Dames:
Bobbie, Sunny, Dorothy and Sue

Dear Reader,

Ron and I (a Dane and a Canuck) always celebrate St Patrick's Day at our favourite restaurant, where we're hosted by an Italian and waited on by a Finn.

It should come as no surprise to you, then, that this St Patrick's Day story brings together a man and a woman who agree on nothing, but who eventually make a celebration of their differences when each is able to provide what the other needs.

Vive la différence! (The Canuck doesn't know how to say that in Gaelic.)

I wish you chocolate shamrocks!

Muriel

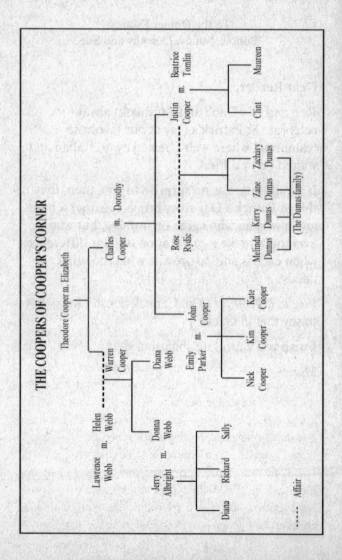

THE COOPERS OF COOPER'S CORNER

Theodore Cooper m. Elizabeth

Charles Cooper — m. Dorothy

Warren Cooper — Diana Webb

Lawrence Webb m. Helen Webb

Donna Webb

Jerry Albright — m. Diana

Diana   Richard   Sally

John Cooper — m. Emily Parker

Nick Cooper   Kim Cooper   Kate Cooper

Justin Cooper — m. Beatrice Tomlin

Clint   Maureen

Rose Rydic

Melinda Dumas   Kerry Dumas   Zane Dumas   Zachary Dumas

(The Dumas family)

- - - - - Affair

CHAPTER ONE

"TELEPHONE, DOCTOR." Julie Freeman, Mike Flynn's office manager, greeted him with the cordless phone as he walked in the door. "It's your wife."

"I don't have a wife," he reminded her, handing her his briefcase so he could pull off his jacket.

She made a face at him. Julie was a pretty brunette in her mid-thirties, the mother of three boys and wife of a cop. It was hard to rattle her.

"You know what I mean," she said softly, holding the phone to her chest as though to protect the caller's sensibilities. "Your ex. And Mrs. Phillips is already here." She lowered her voice. "The twins from hell are in three and four." She handed back his briefcase.

"Thank you." Mike walked toward his office with the phone, remembering how he used to hate it when a day started this way—patients here before he was, a frantic atmosphere in the office when he was determined to take a Zen approach to dentistry.

But he was older and wiser now. Zen had to be modified in a schedule dictated by other people's emergencies, and since Marianne had left with his children two years ago, every day was the same, anyway. In his office, he slapped his briefcase on a chair and went to the window with its aerial view of downtown Boston. He put the phone to his ear. "Yes?" he asked, polite but cool as he watched the early-morning activity.

"Michael," Marianne said sweetly. "How are you?"

"I'm fine, Marianne," he replied in the same cool tone. And in no mood for chitchat, he added silently. "What is it?"

He heard a theatrical gasp of indignation. "Well, you might show a little interest. What if something was wrong with one of the girls?" It amazed him that she continued to expect him to be friendly and forgiving when she'd taken their children and left him without warning for the contractor who'd been doing their renovation. During the divorce proceedings, he'd discovered they'd been lovers for several months. He hated being stupid.

"Claudie called me on her way to school this morning, so I know the girls are all right." Claudette was their eight-year-old. "Whatever the reason for this call, it has to be about you."

She sighed. "So it is. Nardo and I were hoping to go to Provincetown for spring break. His friend runs a gallery there and wants to talk to him about having a show. We were hoping to turn the visit into a romantic getaway if you'll take the girls."

Mike's interest was suddenly piqued. Nardo was an artist, the third boyfriend she'd had since the contractor. According to Claudie, he was Portuguese and nice enough, but strange. He used the garage for a studio, and Marianne was always complaining because when he'd moved his things into it, he'd dragged out the gardening tools and everything else stored in there. It all still stood in the driveway, covered with a tarp.

But their romantic getaway meant he could have Claudie and Angel, five, for longer than a weekend. "Of course I'll take them," he said.

"And Chewie, too? The kennel's booked up."

He smiled. Chewbacca, a one-hundred-and-fifty-pound Saint Bernard, had been Mike's when he married Marianne, but the girls were attached to the dog, so he'd let Marianne have him in the divorce. Mike missed him, though.

"And Chewie."

Mike's condo didn't allow pets, so a week-long visit from the dog meant that he would have to take the girls on a trip. He remembered that Julie and her husband had taken their children and two full-size poodles on a vacation in the Berkshires. He'd have to ask her where they'd stayed.

"You're a dear," Marianne said, her voice breathy and lowered an octave. Was she tiring of the artist already? In the two years since their divorce, she seemed to have been on some kind of self-exploration odyssey. He'd spoken to his lawyer about filing for complete custody of the girls, but he'd been told he didn't have a leg to stand on. Claudie was doing well in school and Angel seemed happy in preschool. There was no evidence that Marianne was a bad mother—just a woman who was indecisive where men were concerned.

So…Mike was biding his time and watching the situation carefully.

Meanwhile, he was delighted at the prospect of having his girls and Chewbacca for eight or nine days.

"Yeah," he said. "I'm a prince. I'll pick them up at nine Saturday morning."

"Perfect. Thank you, Mike."

"Sure. Bye, Marianne."

"Mike?"

He shifted his weight and tried to reply patiently. He had things to do now—block out that week of appointments, find a motel that'd take a Saint Bernard, lay in chocolate-cream-filled cookies for Claudie and Rice Krispies Treats for Angel.

"Yes?" he asked.

"Are you ever going to forgive me?" Her voice was plaintive and wheedling.

"No," he answered, astonished she could even ask the question. "You ruined our lives."

"Because I deceived you and you're embarrassed that I put something over on you." She spoke the words as though convinced it was his problem and not hers.

"Because I trusted you and believed in you," he corrected, "and you stole my children."

There was a moment's silence. "But you see them every other weekend," she argued.

As if that was enough. He had to bite his tongue. He had an office full of people. And she just didn't get it, anyway.

"Is there anything else?" he asked stiffly.

"No," she replied. "Nothing. Goodbye, Mike."

"Goodbye, Marianne." He turned off the phone and took a minute to clear his mind. He'd recovered from her deception, and he was doing fine without her, though not so well without the girls. He had a thriving practice and a reasonably satisfying life. But he'd never let love into it again. He'd learned an important lesson.

That resolved, he walked back to Julie's desk with the phone and asked her to clear next week's appointments. She blinked at him. "The whole week?" She flipped through the appointment book to show him the filled pages.

"I'm getting the girls," he explained. "Just reschedule as best you can."

She understood his devotion to his daughters. "I'll get right on it."

"I'm also getting Chewie." He picked up the files for today's patients. "What's the name of that place where you and Rick and the boys stayed with the dogs?"

She pulled a business card off the bulletin board to her left and handed it to him. "Here you go. Twin

Oaks Bed and Breakfast in Cooper's Corner. You'll love it.''

''And they'll take a Saint Bernard?''

''I'm pretty sure. There was a young couple with a Newfoundland staying the same time we were.''

He studied the card, then handed it back to her. ''Will you book it for me, please? Monday through Saturday.''

''Sure. It's wonderful. Rural setting, rolling hills, church steeples and homes from the 1800s.'' She sighed dreamily. ''Wish I was going back. It was so romantic in the fall.''

''Thanks.'' He didn't need romance, just a place where the girls and the dog could run. He headed for room one and Mrs. Phillips, who was about to begin a teeth-whitening procedure. As he walked by room two, he saw five-year-old Travis Holland standing in the middle of the exam chair, inspecting the drill, while his mother sat nearby reading a magazine.

In room three, Trevor Holland and his father played catch with a can of Carbocaine. He had to talk to Julie about making sure the new assistant remembered to clean up at night before leaving. The Holland twins and their permissive parents drove organized and disciplined Julie crazy, but Mike rather enjoyed them because their little family was so tightly knit.

He envied them that.

''AND THE WINNER OF THE Neighborhood Market's People's Choice Employee of the Year...'' Toby Janeiro, manager of the market and leader of this morning's meeting, smiled tauntingly from the head of the long table in the staff room. Around the table sat six checkers, four box boys, two butchers, the produce manager and the customer-service clerk. They all waited expectantly.

Colleen O'Connor glanced at her watch, wondering if she'd still have time to call her sister before the store opened. Spring break was a mere week away and she still hadn't lined up a sitter for the boys. Their customary sitter was going away for the week, and the drop-in child-care center at the church was booked up. Her younger sister, Jerri, a freelance writer who worked from home, was her only hope.

She would bribe her with chocolate, Colleen strategized. Jerri would do almost anything for peanut clusters.... Her thoughts were interrupted when she realized that everyone was staring at her. Great. Toby had probably asked some question of her as the employee association representative and she'd been caught with her mind wandering.

She sat up brightly, trying to imagine what he'd asked her so she could formulate an answer. Then Barbie Hoyt, another checker, who looked like Mariah Carey and had the worst taste in men, leaned over to give Colleen a hug.

"Congratulations!" she said excitedly. "Imagine! A whole week off on the store!"

"What?" Colleen asked in disbelief.

Toby rolled his eyes. "If you'd pay attention to

me," he teased, waving a sheet of paper in his hand, "instead of using staff meetings to daydream, you'd have heard that you won Employee of the Year by a landslide!"

She gasped in surprise. "I did?"

Her co-workers laughed. They were a good group, friendly and supportive of one another. She'd worked for the Neighborhood Market in New Bedford, Massachusetts, for nearly two years, and though she often dreamed of winning the lottery so she could open her own design studio, she was levelheaded enough to face reality. That wasn't going to happen. And she hadn't had a good idea for a greeting card design or verse in more than a month, anyway, so her ability to supplement her income was currently down the tubes. If she was going to have to work like a dog to support her two boys, she'd just as soon do it where her co-workers were kind and fun to be with.

Toby came around the table to hand her the sheet of paper. "This is confirmation of a week's stay at the Twin Oaks Bed and Breakfast in Cooper's Corner for you and the boys." He handed her a business-size envelope. "And this is some spending money. Thank you, Colleen, for being such a good employee."

Everyone applauded and she smiled her thanks. She looked over the letter, still stunned, then peeked inside the envelope. She saw hundred-dollar bills. Several of them. She was too polite to pull them out and count them.

"Thank you," she said, her voice frail. A week's

vacation at someone else's expense! With cash! She'd
died and gone to heaven. And she wouldn't have to
worry about calling Jerri.

She looked through the brochure that was in the
envelope and saw a beautiful rustic setting, playground equipment, horseback riding nearby. The boys
would be ecstatic and she wouldn't have to worry
about meals or laundry for an entire week.

Maybe she'd come home refreshed enough to feel
creative again. She experienced a little shudder of excitement. She'd never won anything. In fact, as luck
went, except for her two beautiful, healthy sons, hers
was usually bad.

She and her sister had been born to a mother who
died young, leaving them in the care of a kind but
alcoholic father who'd never been sober when they'd
needed him. He'd died, too, when Jerri was a senior
in high school.

Marrying Danny had been a mistake for which Colleen had paid over and over. Thanks to her chro-
nically unemployed husband, there'd never been
enough money to put down on a house or to buy a
car less than ten years old. Since he'd left two years
ago, she'd lost her job as a copywriter for an ad
agency, worked briefly for a small publisher that went
out of business, and delivered newspapers at four
o'clock in the morning to have money to buy groceries. Then she'd come to work at the market.

She lived in a three-bedroom apartment in a con-
verted factory and drove an eleven-year-old Toyota

that was fortunately reliable. She'd had to give up the newspaper delivery job, unwilling to leave the boys alone at that hour.

She had no money for vacations or frivolities of any kind. Whatever clothing budget she squeaked out of her paycheck went to keep her growing boys outfitted. Her own wardrobe was thanks to Jerri's weakness for chocolate, which developed last year when her position was downsized in a merger of marketing firms. The chocolate and sudden free time had caused her to go up a size and pass the clothes she'd outgrown on to her sister.

A week away! Colleen couldn't believe it. Then she remembered the cat. She'd have to board Fu Manchu. Of course, Colleen had been asked not to return to the kennel where she'd boarded the cat when she had accompanied the Boy Scouts on a camping trip. The cat had apparently terrorized all the other animals—dogs included—and given the owner of the kennel a very rakish scar.

Maybe she'd have to call Jerri, after all.

Then she noticed the line in bold print on the bottom of the brochure. Your Pets Welcome, Too! No! She couldn't believe it. Even that little detail was in her favor.

She accepted the congratulations of her friends as the clock struck eight and they all went to begin their duties. Was her luck changing? She was afraid to think so.

The little part of her that remained cynical despite

the Pollyanna front she put on for her children and the world wouldn't let her quite believe that. But she proceeded cheerfully, anyway. Something had happened in her favor, however temporary, and that was remarkable.

"BUT I THOUGHT YOU WERE going to see if Aunt Jerri would watch us for spring break," Bill complained as Colleen folded several pairs of his cords into a suitcase. Bill was eight and complained about everything. He wasn't deliberately difficult, just at an analytical stage where nothing could be taken at face value or considered in a positive light. "What if we don't like this Double Oaks place?"

"It's not Double Oaks, it's Twin Oaks," she corrected, "and I really need to get away somewhere quiet, so you're going to love it. I insist." She kissed his cheek as she passed him on the way to his closet. "You want to bring your Boston Red Sox sweatshirt?"

"I want to bring my Bugs Bunny one!" Bugsy shouted from the bottom of the closet, where he dug for boots.

"I knew that, Bugs," Colleen replied, snatching Bill's Red Sox sweatshirt and the hooded gray one that was his second favorite. Justin had been nicknamed "Bugsy" when he was two because of his affection for the clever cartoon rabbit. Thanks to his aunt, he had every Bugs Bunny-patterned piece of clothing available.

Bill took the Red Sox shirt from her. "I have to have something to wear in the car." He frowned. "But what are we going to do there? Aunt Jerri always lets me use her exercise stuff when we stay with her."

Jerri had every piece of gym equipment known to man, but Colleen was still getting her hand-me-downs, so she could only guess her sister wasn't using the machines as often as she should. But Colleen thought Jerri's extra twenty pounds gave her a soft roundness that was a nice change from the angular, anxious dynamo she used to be.

"The brochure shows playground equipment," Colleen said cheerfully, folding the hooded sweatshirt into the bag.

Bill put socks in with a desultory toss. "That's for babies." He sank onto the bed, disgruntled. He had his father's rich brown hair, freckled face and ability to make Colleen feel guilty when she couldn't provide every single thing he wanted.

She sat down beside him and put an arm around his shoulders. He shifted away from her stiffly.

"I'm sorry you're disappointed about not going to Aunt Jerri's," she said gently. "I'm sorry I can't always do everything you want, but the unfortunate truth about life is that you get what you want only about fifty percent of the time—and that's if you're lucky. The other fifty, you learn to be happy with what you get."

He folded his arms, still resisting her touch. "So you're always just fifty percent happy?"

"No," she replied, pulling him closer. "I'm one hundred percent happy, because I have you and Bugs."

He sighed and leaned into her. "But Dad left."

She squeezed him. "I know. But when he wasn't happy being here, it put my happy percentage in the negative zone. Have you learned about that in math yet?"

"Just a little. It means less than zero, right?"

Less than zero. That aptly described the last year of their marriage before Danny left.

"Right. He took away from our life as a family rather than added to it because he wasn't happy to be here. He wanted to be free to do what *he* wanted to do."

Bill sighed. "He's only about ten percent happy most of the time. I mean, he laughs and jokes and all, but when he has to really do stuff, he isn't happy."

Colleen kissed him again for that astute observation. "*That* doesn't mean he doesn't love you, just that he's not family material."

"Other fathers stay around. How come we didn't get one of those?"

Because I was lonely and not careful to look beyond charm and flattery, she thought. She wondered how to explain that to an eight-year-old.

"Because I was very young when I married him," she explained, "and I thought that the same things that made someone fun at football games and dances would make them good at being part of a family. But that wasn't true."

"'Cause life isn't all about having fun, right?"

"Right."

"Dad didn't even call for my birthday."

"I know. I'm sorry." She held him closer, thinking she'd do anything to be able to change the past and give him the father he deserved. "He probably got busy...."

"He just forgot. But it's okay." He wrapped both arms around her. "I really liked the pizza party and the sleepover. And we can still be maybe ninety percent happy even though he isn't here."

"Ninety percent's pretty good," she said, drawing back to smile at him. "I can do ninety."

"Yeah, me, too."

Bugsy came toward the smaller case standing open beside Bill's, an armload of clothes crushed against him. On the top was one bright yellow boot decorated with eyes and a duck bill. "I can't find the other one," he complained to Colleen. "Ha! Look what's in my bag, Mom!"

Colleen and Bill both went around to the foot of the bed to see what had brought Bugsy to giggles.

It was Fu Manchu, the two-year-old cat Colleen had rescued from the animal shelter when Danny moved out. Not that a pet could come close to replacing a father, but she'd thought it important that the boys have something else to think about.

A litter of half Siamese and half something else that had surprised a breeder's kennel had been left at the shelter. Chuie, a female, looked like a purebred and had an attitude to match. Her mother was a Silver Point, and Chuie had inherited the rich silver coat, the black-tipped ears and big blue eyes. Her limbs were long and graceful and she extended one now toward the boys.

Adore me, the gesture said. *I can take it.*

"What about Chuie?" Bugsy asked as Bill nuzzled the cat. "Where's she gonna go while we're gone?"

"She's going to come with us," Colleen said. "She'll have lots of fun, too."

Bill scooped the cat out of Bugsy's bag and placed her over his shoulder, where she loved to drape. She sank against him bonelessly, purring.

Bill laughed. "Chuie must think she has one hundred percent of what she wants," he said to Colleen. "Or else she's learned to be happy with what she's got, too."

CHAPTER TWO

"IF YOU'RE HAPPY AND YOU know it, clap your hands!" Claudie and Angel sang from the van's second seat as Mike drove north on 7, somewhere between Pittsfield and Williamstown, headed for Cooper's Corner. They clapped as the song demanded, then sang the next line, a repetition of the first.

He smiled at the road and decided that his quickly blossoming headache was a small price to pay for the raucous good cheer taking place behind him. His daughters were beautiful and brilliant, but even he had to admit that their voices were off-key. What they lacked in purity of sound, they made up for in volume.

"If you're happy and you know it, and you really want to show it..." They continued at full volume as he drove along the quiet, tree-lined road. A loud bark erupted from the back, where Chewie was confined behind a pet-safety gate.

He hated being separated from the girls and had protested repeatedly during the trip. Or perhaps he was singing along. Mike wasn't entirely sure which.

"It's okay Chewie," he called to the dog, spotting

his mournful face in the rearview mirror. "We're almost there. About ten minutes."

"If you're happy and you know it, stamp your feet!"

Mike ignored the cheerful chorus and the whining dog to concentrate on the road sign ahead.

"Welcome to Cooper's Corner," it read. "Heart of the Berkshires."

Mike knew this area was beautiful in the fall. Oaks, maples and white pines lived in colorful crowds and ran up the hillsides, which were aesthetically dotted with church steeples and smoke rising from chimneys.

Now, however, it was almost mid-March. The deciduous trees were bare, and rain fell with ark-building vehemence. Earth and sky were gray, lending a monochromatic simplicity to everything in between.

Cooper's Corner, however, shone like a pretty little duck in the deluge as Mike drove through. They passed homes from the 1800s, some surrounded by equally old stone walls, and newer homes built in the same style.

"There's a park!" Angel said excitedly, then added in disappointment, "but no swings. Just that guy."

"That guy" was a bronze statue of a young Revolutionary War soldier in waistcoat and breeches, rifle at his side.

"That's a village green," Claudie corrected. She'd been convinced since her little sister was born that she'd been created solely for the purpose of educating her. "Like we have in Boston. You know. Boston Common. Where Charlie used to play football on Sunday afternoon when you and me and Mom went to buy ice cream."

Charlie had been boyfriend number two.

"Yeah," Angel replied. "The park. But who's the guy?"

"I don't know. Who's the soldier, Dad?"

"Not sure," he replied. "Probably a minuteman, but I don't know who specifically."

He spotted the sign for Twin Oaks Bed and Breakfast at the foot of a tree-lined drive and turned onto it.

"We can investigate who he is when we go to town for dinner," he said. "Meanwhile...look! We're here."

A large farmhouse stood on a knoll in the middle of what the brochure said was one hundred and sixty acres. He pulled up to the front porch as rain beat against the windshield and obscured his view of what he was sure was a beautiful place.

Claudie ripped off her seat belt and opened her door. Angel was right behind her. Chewie barked anxiously from the back of the car.

"Hold on, Chewie," Mike shouted as he, too, climbed out of the van. "We'll be right back for you."

The girls raced up the steps to an oak door with a leaded glass window and huddled under the shelter of the porch overhang until he caught up with them.

He pushed the door open and ushered them inside. They clung to his side as they entered a quiet foyer. The wood floors shone, and light from a lamp on the front desk picked out highlights in the old wood and family pictures on the wall. There were lace curtains at the windows, and beyond them the afternoon light, trapped behind pewter clouds, was already waning. The place smelled of furniture polish and good house-keeping.

"Hello!" an attractive young woman greeted them from behind the desk. "What an afternoon to be trav-eling! You must be the Flynns."

"How did you know that?" Angel asked.

"Because Daddy made reservations," Claudie re-plied. "We're staying for a whole week."

"Yes, I know," the woman said. "We're very happy to have you. Did you know that it's supposed to snow before the week is out?"

Angel jumped up and down. "Do you have a sled?"

"I have three."

"Wow!"

Mike approached the desk, already feeling his stress level lower just a little.

"Welcome to Twin Oaks," the woman said, offer-ing her hand. "I'm Maureen Cooper."

Mike was grateful that he'd sworn off women for the rest of his life. This one could make him think twice. She was tall and pretty, with long, chestnut-brown hair caught up in a ponytail and green eyes filled with honesty and charm. She wore soft, worn beige cords and a blue-and-beige sweater.

"Michael Flynn," he said, handing her his credit card. She walked back around the desk. "Can you tell me what the rules are regarding the dog?"

She gave him a slip of paper to sign, then handed him a key. "The dog can go anywhere you do in the house, as long as he's with you. It's best to leave him in the room while we're having breakfast, though. But if you're planning to sit in the living room, you're welcome to bring him down. We have another pet visiting this weekend, so we ask only that you work out an amicable arrangement if they don't get along."

"Sounds reasonable."

"And there are other children, too," she told Angel and Claudie.

Claudie brightened. "Girls?"

Maureen shook her head. "Two boys."

Claudie stuck her tongue out in a *yuck!* gesture.

"Claudette!" Mike scolded with a laugh. "Men make up half the population. If there weren't any boys, there wouldn't be any dads."

She was unimpressed with his argument. "Dads are okay. Boys are gross."

"Gross?" That teasingly indignant exclamation came from a man about Mike's age, walking down the stairs with two identical little girls younger than Angel. "*All* boys?"

"All boys." Claudie held her position. "But not dads," she offered as a peacemaker.

"Well, I hope not," the man said as he and the little girls reached the desk. "You're going to hurt my feelings."

Maureen came around the counter. "Mike, Claudie and Angel Flynn," she said, "I'd like you to meet my brother and partner in the bed-and-breakfast, Clint Cooper, and my daughters, Randi and Robin Cooper."

Mike shook Clint's hand. The man had a good four or five inches on him, and the easy confidence that probably came from being bigger and taller than almost everyone around him.

"Good to meet you," Mike said. "It's a beautiful place." He smiled at the twins. "Claudie and Angel will be happy to have other girls to play with."

The twins were beautiful replicas of their mother, with remarkable blue-green eyes. They wore jeans and sweatshirts, and their ponytails were askew as they jumped up and down.

"It's gonna snow!" Randi said.

"Today!" Robin added.

"Not today, girls, but very soon." Maureen pushed them gently toward the kitchen. "You go get your cookies and ask Keegan to pour you some milk, okay? He's peeling potatoes."

"Your room's all ready," Clint told Mike. "The girls and I just checked it out. I hope you enjoy your stay. If you'll excuse me, I have some things in the oven."

Maureen nodded toward her brother as he left the

room. "Clint's our chef." Then she pointed toward the stairs. "You're overlooking the vegetable garden. Not much to see right now, I'm afraid, but if it snows, the view will be spectacular from every room."

"Thank you. Okay, girls. Let's go check things out, then we'll get the bags and the dog and settle in."

The girls scampered on ahead of Mike, giggling. They stomped like stevedores up the stairs.

Mike smiled at Maureen apologetically. "They're a little excited," he explained. "They'll quiet down once we're settled in."

She laughed. "You saw my twins. I haven't had a quiet day since the girls were born. Please don't apologize, just enjoy your stay."

"Thanks again." He followed Claudie and Angel, already liking it here. He felt confident that he and the girls would have some good bonding time together, and he'd be able to shed the curious disquiet he was always aware of but couldn't quite define. It had started when Marianne left with the girls and had grown slowly since.

He knew he couldn't blame anyone for it. The world was filled with divorced people who were separated from their children and found a way to cope. He had to do it, too.

A week at Twin Oaks was going to restore the old Mike Flynn, for whom nothing was impossible. He felt a surge of adrenaline fill him as he hurried up the stairs.

COLLEEN WAS IN HEAVEN. She loved the shiny, hardwood floors she hadn't had to polish, the chocolate chip cookies the boys were eating that she didn't have to bake, the broad expanse of lawn outside. She'd hardly even seen grass since they'd moved into their apartment two years ago.

She stared out the kitchen window as she opened a can of cat food.

Chuie, who hadn't been too pleased about the long drive in the car, now sat with the boys in a small sunporch off the kitchen. Rain beat against the windows, but the cat didn't seem to mind as she perched on a wide windowsill, happy to be free of her carrier.

Colleen spooned the cat food into Chuie's plastic bowl and headed for the sunporch, calling, "Here, Chuie! Come and get it!"

MIKE AND THE GIRLS were just coming back into the foyer after retrieving the dog and their bags when Maureen called them toward her. She came around the desk, leaning down to admire the dog.

"Well, you're a handsome devil," she said to Chewie, who reacted with slobbering, tail-wagging ecstasy.

Maureen handed him a dog biscuit, which he ate noisily and with great relish. "What a sweetheart!" she exclaimed, petting the rich brown-and-white coat. "He doesn't look like he's going to be any trouble."

Those words had just been spoken when Mike heard a cheerful command in another lilting female voice. "Here, Chuie! Come and get it!"

He couldn't quite believe his ears.

He didn't even have time to wonder what was going on when Chewie yanked away from him and set off in the direction of the voice calling his name.

"Chewie!" Mike shouted, following at a run.

But the dog, confined for so many hours and hungry, was not about to be deterred from his objective. His tendency to carsickness always meant no dinner until they'd reached their destination.

Mike heard screams before he made it to the kitchen. He skidded to a halt in the doorway of a sunporch, where Chewie had pinned a slender victim to the floor and appeared to be eating her pale red hair. The soles of small tennis shoes pedaled the air.

Oh, God.

COLLEEN HAD LIVED IN Massachusetts her entire life and could not remember experiencing one earthquake. Yet she stopped still as the ground began to shake and she heard a thundering sound.

Before she could even analyze what it could possibly be, something brown and white and very large with frenzied eyes was sailing through the air at her.

She screamed, the bowl flew, and she fell on her back with a bone-rattling thud, certain she was about to be eaten by an apparently carnivorous guernsey.

She screamed again as it licked her face, then chewed on her hair, clearly some tenderizing ritual before it ate the rest of her. Great. Why couldn't she have been eaten on the *last* day of her vacation?

"Oh, my God!" An anxious male voice hovered somewhere above her, but she couldn't see anything but tongue and horrifyingly large teeth.

"Chewie, up!" the voice shouted.

A corner of Colleen's mind not occupied with terror wondered why the man was calling her cat.

"Chewie! Chewie, come on! Get…off!" There was a grunt, and the crushing weight was suddenly lifted off her.

But before she could appreciate the ability to breathe again, there was Chuie's unmistakable screech, followed by a deep-throated bark, then all hell broke loose in the small sunporch.

Growls and whines filled the air. Colleen sat up just in time to see an enormous dog leaping and writhing around the room, Chuie attached to his back. A wicker chair fell over and the boys shouted. Bill rescued a pot of flowers from the wicker coffee table just before it fell onto its side.

A man chased the dog in the confined space, finally catching his collar and pulling him to a stop. "Chewie, it's okay," he said, patting the whining dog's head. "It's okay."

Bill snatched the cat from the dog's back while she hissed her displeasure at the disruption of her nap.

Two beautiful little girls ran to the dog, the oldest one saying worriedly, "His ear's bleeding, Daddy!"

The man leaned over the dog to inspect the wound.

Sitting on a scratchy sisal rug and smelling of chicken giblets and tuna, Colleen surveyed the worried tableau. Knowing her luck, there was sure to be a lawsuit. The Saint Bernard was probably a show dog, resting between appearances at Westminster.

"It's not very deep. If Maureen has hydrogen peroxide, we can fix that right up." He turned to Bill, who was petting a still-hissing Chuie. "The cat okay?" he asked.

Bill nodded. "I think so. She's just mad. But she's always mad."

The man seemed suddenly to remember Colleen and came back to her, catching her hands and pulling her to her feet. The action was swift, certain—and a little startling.

"I'm so sorry!" he said, running diagnostic hands down her arms. "Are you all right?"

She was angry, embarrassed and...and...something else. Something that was a reaction to his stroking hands—however clinically he'd intended the gesture—and the downright gorgeousness of his person.

He had short black hair, unusually dark blue eyes, a strong, straight nose, and a square chin with a slight cleft in it.

She knew she was staring, and that somehow intensified her anger and embarrassment.

"No, I'm not all right!" she said, pulling free of his hold. "I was just attacked by...by..." She pointed in the direction of the dog. "Certainly that doesn't qualify as a pet! It could be ridden!"

He drew a breath, apparently determined to remain calm.

"Chewie is a dog," he said reasonably, "and he is a little big, but you were calling his name and carrying food. He can't be blamed for…"

"Chewie?" she asked in disbelief. "Your dog's name is Chewie?"

"Chewbacca," he explained. "You know, the Wookie in…"

She tilted her head impatiently. "I know who Chewbacca is. I was calling my cat, not your dog."

He raised an eyebrow. It was beautifully arched, she noticed. "Your cat's name is Chewbacca?"

"Fu Manchu," Bill put in. "We call her Chuie, too. We know it's a guy's name, but we got her from the shelter and they had already named her. We tried to call her Daisy, but she wouldn't come."

The man turned to look at the cat, who was now grooming with apparent urgency, as though she'd just dealt with the unclean and had to purge herself of their effect.

"No, she doesn't look like a Daisy," he said. Then he offered his hand to Bill. "I'm Mike Flynn," he said.

Bill looked first surprised, then flattered by the adult gesture. He put his small hand in the large one. "I'm Bill O'Connor. That's my brother, Bugsy."

Bugs came over to shake hands and was treated with the same male acceptance. Colleen was ridiculously pleased for her boys. They had relatively little adult male contact in their lives and she felt guilty about it. She felt guilty about everything.

"This is my mom," Bill said, pointing to her. "Her name's Colleen."

She saw the look in Mike Flynn's eyes change when he turned to her. It seemed to say that while he was sorry for what had happened, he was through apologizing. She should accept that it had been an accident and let it go.

Unfortunately, she was at a point in her life where she was tired of having to accept life's inequities with grace and silence. Her new sweater was ruined and someone was going to have to make that up to her.

She opened her mouth to tell him he was going to have to pay for the sweater, when he offered his hand and said, "I'm sorry about your clothes. I'll replace them for you." Then his eyes went from her torn sweater to her hair. "And…your hair."

Her hair. She remembered then that the dog had been chewing on it, so it probably contained the chicken giblets and tuna that also covered her blouse. Was it sticking up? she wondered. Was she standing here arguing with a gorgeous man while her very short hair stood up in points, moussed with cat food?

She was sure she might laugh about this later, but she failed to see the humor in it at the moment.

"Never mind," she said stiffly, going to the windowsill for Chuie. Calmer, the cat allowed herself to be picked up without complaint. "You've done enough for now. We'll just excuse ourselves, if you don't mind.''

"Oh, please don't go!" Maureen stood in the doorway to the sunporch, an ambassadorial smile on her face. "I have peroxide to fix Chewie's ear right up," she said. "I can give the cat a bowl of cream to make amends, and Clint just took an apple pie out of the oven. Why don't the six of you sit down at the table and start over with pie à la mode?''

The boys looked at her hopefully, but she wasn't staying down here another moment. And she couldn't very well leave them to enjoy the pie without her supervision.

She smiled politely at Maureen. "Thank you, but I think I'd better get cleaned up and find something else to wear." That last was added in a long-suffering tone.

"You could leave the boys with us," Mike Flynn said pleasantly, a silent message in his voice, too. "So they don't have to miss the pie." *While you're pouting,* it said.

"Thank you," she replied stiffly, "but I never leave the boys anywhere. Bill. Bugsy."

She started for the stairs and heard the grumbling boys follow her.

"Never get to do anything."

"Never get to have pie."

"Never get to have fun."

"Wish we could go home."

"COLLEEN SEEMS REALLY FUN and nice to be with," Maureen said as she scooped vanilla ice cream onto the slices of apple pie she'd placed before Mike and the girls at a large mahogany dining table. After feeding him, Mike had taken Chewie up to their room and confined him in the bathroom for safety's sake. "I'm sure she was just reacting to being stood on by one hundred and fifty pounds of dog."

"You know her?" Mike asked. He didn't really want to know her himself, but he remembered that she was rather small, though nicely round, and very pretty in a pixieish sort of way.

He took a bite of pie, unable to believe he'd entertained that thought. Pixieish. He'd never cared for small, perky women. He liked them tall and lush, capable and mysterious.

But then, Marianne had fit that description, and all she'd turned out to be capable of was attracting other men, and the only mystery involved there was what the hell had happened to his life?

"No, I didn't know her before she and the boys arrived last night," Maureen said. "But she's warm and friendly, and now I feel as though I've known her forever."

He cast her an amused glance as she sat across the table from them with her own slice of pie. "Warm and friendly, huh?" he asked dryly.

"Well, Chewie did knock her to the ground and eat tuna out of her hair."

Claudie laughed. When Mike gave her a silencing look, she said loyally, "It wasn't Daddy's fault. She was calling Chewie's name."

Maureen nodded. "Yes. It was all a very unfortunate misunderstanding. But I'd take it as a personal favor if you won't hold it against her. She won her stay here because she was voted employee of the year at the store where she works in New Bedford. She has to be a nice person."

"She's pretty!" Angel said, feet dangling from her chair as she attacked her pie with enthusiasm. "But her hair's funny. Kinda orange!"

"That's called strawberry blond," Claudie corrected, "not orange."

Whatever it was called, Mike thought, it had been pretty spectacular, even spiked with tuna. It had looked a little like the flame of a candle.

She had beautiful eyes, too, a jade color with a darker shade of green surrounding the iris. He'd never seen anything like them. They contributed to the pixie impression; if you came upon her in the woods, one look from her could turn you into some other lifeform.

He tuned out as Maureen and the girls talked about hair. He ate his pie and tried not to think about how long it had been since he'd made love to a woman. Right after his divorce he'd been angry at all women, and taken a certain satisfaction in liaisons where nothing more was expected of him than performance. He'd enjoyed proving that he was good, then moving on.

That thrill was short-lived and he soon became disgusted with himself and the circle of beautiful, high-powered women who'd accommodated him. When he wasn't at the office or with his daughters, he became reclusive.

But he hadn't the talent for celibacy. He was neither happy in his solitude, nor satisfied with his decision never to make love again rather than do it out of retribution or boredom or for entertainment purposes.

He ached all the time. He maintained a caring but removed attitude with those single female patients who'd have been happy to relieve him of his loneliness, and a friendly but not interested demeanor with the women he'd dated after his divorce who kept calling. Inside, he longed for something to change.

Still, he didn't want a coldhearted, sharp-tongued pixie who couldn't see the humor in a situation. Of course, the dog had frightened her, but once Mike had apologized and explained, she could have been a little more gracious. It wasn't as though Chewie had deliberately attacked her.

She'd done what so many women did—blamed the nearest man for whatever was wrong in her life.

No. He didn't want to have to deal with a wife's continuous complaints ever again, no matter how much he missed the middle-of-the-night intimacy, having someone to share a laugh or a thought with, having his children actually live in the same house he lived in…

God. He was a family man trapped in a bachelor's life and he hated it.

"I STILL DON'T SEE WHY we couldn't have had the pie," Bill said for the tenth time as Colleen drove cautiously in the darkness, searching for the Burger Barn. Maureen had told her it was just a short distance out of town.

"There, Mom!" Bill shouted from the back seat. "See the big neon sign?"

She did. She turned into the parking lot just ahead and pulled into a spot right beside the entrance. "Bill, could you please get over the pie," she said, unbuckling her seat belt and reaching for her jacket. "You can have whatever you want for dessert here, okay? I was just in no mood for pie and small talk after having a horse standing on my chest."

"You had tuna in your hair," Bill reminded with a giggle as he pushed open his door.

"Thank you," she said sweetly. "I'd almost managed to forget that." She saw lights coming up behind her in her rearview mirror, probably heading for the parking spot beside them. "Bugsy," she called quickly, "wait for me before you get out."

"I'm gonna have French fries and a hot fudge sundae!" Bugsy was out of his seat belt and pushing the back door open, her order missed in his excitement to get out of the car.

She reached an arm over the back of her seat and caught the sleeve of his jacket just as she heard the squeal of brakes. Or was it her own squeal as she watched her right rear side door crumple like an accordion as a large van hit it.

Bugsy screamed, and for one horrible moment she thought the van had hit him.

"He's okay, Mom!" Bill assured her, scrambling across the seat to his brother. "See? Two legs inside the car. He just got scared. Wow, look at the door! That's so cool!"

Colleen, still dealing with shock, leapt out the driver's side and ran around the back of her car to get to her son and assess the damage.

But Mike Flynn had gotten there before her. For an instant she couldn't figure out why, until she saw his daughters sitting in the van that was now attached to her car door. It was his.

"You okay, Bugs?" he asked. He was on one knee beside the open door, his hands on her son's shoulders. "Did I hit you?"

Bugsy shook his head frantically, a small smile appearing on his face. "No. Just the door. Wow! It's just like the Terror-Trucks commercial. Pow! Crunch!" Bugsy punched the air in imitation of the advertisement for the toy.

Mike spotted her standing nearby and caught Bugsy's fist in his own. "Cool it, pal," he cautioned quietly. "I don't think your mom's going to want to hear sound effects."

He got to his feet, closed his eyes a moment as though he couldn't quite believe what had happened, then opened them and focused on her. "I'm sorry," he said with a sigh. "I didn't have time to stop."

She hated to admit it, but she knew he wasn't at fault. Still—it was clear there was some destructive force traveling with him, destined to destroy her. This was going to cost her a fortune she didn't have. She couldn't afford collision insurance and carried only liability.

She swallowed until she could trust herself to speak calmly. "I know." Panic was erupting inside her. This free trip was going to cost her a mint. "It was our fault."

He seemed surprised by that admission. "I'll take it to a garage for you first thing in the morning," he offered.

She shook her head. "My insurance doesn't cover collision. I'll have to…" What did she have to do? Drive it home this way? Go all the way back to New Bedford with the back of the car open?

He was apparently reading her mind. "You can't do that," he insisted. "You drive home with it like this and the boys will freeze and you'll be fair game for anyone capable of reaching inside and…"

"Please!" she screamed at him. Then, realizing she was losing it, she swallowed again and said with deliberate calm, "Please. I can formulate my own horror scenarios, thank you. Now, if you'll just leave us alone, we'll go inside and have dinner."

He reached out to take her arm. "Come on, I'll buy you dinner, then we'll take you back to Twin Oaks."

She tried to pull away from him. "No, thank you. There's some poisonous karma surrounding you that's determined to get me."

He held on. "That's silly," he scolded. "It was an accident."

She looked into his eyes, belligerence in hers. "I've had two since I met you," she said, "and that was only three hours ago. I don't think it's safe to risk spending any more time with you. Now, if you'll excuse us…"

"I'll call the police and report it," he said.

"Good," she replied. "If they need me, I'll be inside."

Colleen enjoyed a completely strange sense of abandon. She let the boys order everything they wanted. Bugsy had his French fries and hot fudge sundae without a meat course, and she let Bill's onion rings pass as a vegetable. She had a deluxe burger with bacon *and* cheese, and never stopped to count the calories or grams of fat.

Maybe her life wasn't going down the tubes, but it sure as hell wasn't getting any easier, even when she'd been gifted with a free, week-long getaway. She was suddenly tired of struggling to hold it all together.

The boys were delighted about the crunched door and talked about it through dinner while Colleen watched Mike's girls come in and order burgers to take out to the van.

Through the window, she saw the police arrive, then after a while they came into the restaurant. She waved them over, gave them all the required information, then sat with curious calm while the boys finished their sundaes.

"Are we gonna drive back to the hotel without the door?" Bill asked eagerly.

"Yes, we are," she said. "You're going to sit up front with me, and Bugsy's going to sit where you usually sit."

"Aw, Mo-om! I want to sit in the back," Bill complained. "I want to see everything go by without the door!"

"Sorry. Come on. Don't forget your jacket."

"Well, how come he gets to sit in the back?" Bill demanded with a disgusted look at his brother.

"Because you're bigger, and if we have an accident and the air bag deploys, you're more likely to survive." She knew he'd love the suggestion of gory possibilities.

"Oh," he said interestedly. "You think the air bag might deploy?"

"Not unless I have an accident."

Colleen pushed through the door into the parking lot—and stopped when she saw Mike Flynn leaning back against the hood of his van, sipping from a paper cup. His girls knelt on the front seats, looking out the windshield.

He straightened when he saw her and dug into his jacket pocket. He held up a ring of keys. "If you'll drive my van back with all the kids," he said, "I'll follow in your car."

"Didn't I just tell you that I'll—" she began hotly, then stopped, realizing that her boys and his girls were staring at her worriedly. She started again in a quieter tone. "Thank you. That's very kind of you. I appreciate your concern, but I can…"

He stopped listening about halfway through her reply and slid the side door open. "Come on, guys," he said, waving her boys inside. "We've got TV in the van."

"Cartoons!" Bugsy exclaimed, and he and Bill piled into the back seat, the girls moving to the middle one.

Colleen watched them with a sense of betrayal. What happened to wanting to watch the road go by without the door?

Mike slid the door closed, then came to the front of the van, where she stood stubbornly. "Colleen," he said quietly, but with an edge of annoyance that was unmistakable. "It's late, I've been driving most of the day, and I'm really not in the mood to deal with a heroic display of female independence. I know you're capable of driving back to the B and B alone. You're probably even capable of replacing your own car door while baking muffins and painting your house with your free hand, but I'm just trying to help, since I feel partially responsible for what happened. Your boys will be safer in my van than in the back of an open car."

Bill, apparently eavesdropping, stuck his head out

a partly open side window. "I was going to sit in the front with her 'cause if the air bag deployed it could kill Bugsy, but not me 'cause I'm bigger."

Mike nodded gravely. "A fine example of a doting mother's concern," he said to Colleen.

She opened her mouth to explain that when she told Bill that, she was using it to make him feel less disappointed and more heroic. Instead, she snatched the keys from him. "We'll do it *your* way," she bargained, "if you promise to keep out of *my* way for the rest of the week!"

"It's a free country," he said, holding his hand out for her keys. "Or didn't you know that?"

She ignored him, delving into her purse for her keys. Unable to find them, she pulled out wallet, checkbook, hair brush, cosmetics bag, map.

She was still routing through a side pocket with a mounting sense of helplessness when he ducked down to look inside her car.

"They're in the ignition," he said, opening the door to his van. "Good place to leave them in an open car."

"Oh, shut up!" she wanted to snap at him, agitated to the point of explosion. But all the children were watching. She felt as though everything inside her simmered and sizzled and was ready to ignite. Even her boys at their worst seldom upset her to this degree.

Mike stepped aside so she could climb into the van.

Colleen put a hand to her eyes, drew a breath and accepted that setting an example for the children came first. "Thank you," she said stiffly, then added under her breath, "If you would stop talking to me, I'd be so grateful."

"My pleasure," he replied. "Need a boost up?"

"I'm sure I can manage, thank you." She tossed her purse in between the front seats, reached for a handgrip above the door, then raised her foot a good eighteen inches to the narrow running board. It wasn't until she tried to pull herself up that she realized her upper-body strength needed work.

She dangled there for a few seconds, then Mike, reaching for her waist but unable to find it in the bulky jacket, put a broad palm to her right hip and pushed. She landed in the driver's seat with a thud.

If she felt explosive before, now her heart was pumping rocket fuel. "How *dare* you!" she breathed angrily.

"Relax," he said, handing her the seat belt. "I'm a doctor."

She was momentarily distracted by that detail. "You are?"

"Well, I'm a dentist," he amended with a grin. "Close enough. See you at Twin Oaks." He closed the door before she could reply.

CHAPTER THREE

As COLLEEN STARTED the engine, Mike's oldest girl leaned over her to hit a few controls on the dashboard and the television went on just behind Colleen's head.

"Get your seat belt on, sweetie," Colleen said, feeling as though she had to retain some control over the situation.

The girl hurried back to her seat, there was a click, and she called, "I'm in!"

Colleen tried to forget her anger and concentrate on driving the tank of a vehicle home. She felt a little like Sandra Bullock in *Speed*. She drove under sixty miles an hour, but the van was so much bigger and more powerful than her little import that she felt as though the lives of her children and Mike's hung in the balance.

A small crowd of women was milling around a Mercedes when Colleen turned into the B and B's parking area. They were pulling bags out of the back of the car, distributing them around the group. When Mike parked beside her, they all stopped and gaped at the sight of the crumpled door.

Colleen didn't hear what he said to the women as

he climbed out of the car, but they laughed, eyeing him with appreciation and clear feminine admiration. One woman in particular, younger than the other three, said something in reply. She and Mike exchanged a few words, then she offered her hand, apparently introducing herself.

She looked like his type, Colleen thought. She was tall, elegant and gracefully smooth in every gesture. Colleen had always wanted to be like that, but her small stature and her basic reluctance to put herself forward got in the way.

She felt curiously jealous and was disgusted with herself for it.

Once she leapt out of the van, she walked around to help the children out.

"That van is so-o-o cool!" Bill said, jumping down beside her. "Why can't we have one?"

"Costs more than we have," Colleen replied with a smile. "But you come up with the money and we'll get one."

"Could we sell Bugsy?"

"Well, he's priceless to me, but not big enough to be worth much on the open market."

"Okay. Well, I'll work on a plan."

"You do that."

"I like your hair," Claudie said to Colleen as she jumped down. "And Daddy says your eyes look like you do magic."

Colleen was at a loss for a reply.

"But he thinks you're cranky. And Mom was always cranky. She didn't think we had enough money."

"Um…well, it takes a lot of money to pay all the bills." Considering the way Danny had been, she might be able to sympathize with the ex-Mrs. Flynn. But it was hard to imagine a dentist being short of funds. Still, everyone had problems other people couldn't see.

"Mom thinks she's going to have to sell the house 'cause Nardo isn't making any money."

"Nardo?"

"Her boyfriend. He's an artist."

Colleen wasn't sure what had inspired this sudden confidence, but Claudie seemed comfortable talking to her. The boys had run over to join Mike, who was still conversing with the beautiful brunette, so Colleen directed the girls toward the B and B.

"I hope we get to live with Daddy," Claudie went on. "Nardo's nice, but he doesn't know much about school stuff, and if we try to watch the Naughty Channel, he doesn't even notice."

"Mmm. But you're smart enough to know you shouldn't, right?"

"Yeah. And I don't get it, anyway. It's just a lot of wrestling and screaming. How come you got divorced?"

"Oh…Bill and Bugsy's dad didn't really like being with us. So he left."

Claudie frowned. "Bill and Bugsy are okay. I mean, for boys."

Colleen had to laugh. "Yes, I think so, too."

Angel caught Colleen's hand as they stopped inside the entryway to wait for Mike and the boys, who were still chatting with the beautiful woman. Colleen noted wryly that even men in the formative stages were attracted to that elegant style.

"How come you don't have any little girls?" Angel asked.

Colleen shrugged. "Probably the same reason your dad doesn't have any little boys. Because you have to take what you get."

Angel nodded. "And you get them at the hospital," she informed them, proud of her knowledge.

Claudie tugged on Colleen's hand until she leaned down to her. "She doesn't understand the whole sex thing," she whispered.

"Mmm." Colleen often thought she didn't understand it, either. After making her life miserable for the last two years of their marriage, Danny had wanted to make love with her "for old times' sake" the day he left. She'd pushed him out the front door and locked it. Cell-splitting, like amoebas, seemed a more sensible approach to procreation.

Colleen turned to the door instinctively to keep an eye on her boys and felt a missed heartbeat as they approached with Mike. The three were laughing about something and the boys looked lighthearted and happy. She hadn't seen them that way in a while.

They were usually pleasant, mostly cooperative, but they'd lost some of their laughter when Danny left.

She felt herself smile.

MIKE STOPPED IN HIS TRACKS just inside the front door. This was the first time he'd seen Colleen O'Connor without a frown. She stood in the foyer with his girls clinging to her, a slender column of denim and quilted fleece, an expression on her face so tender it struck right at his heart. And she was looking at *him!*

He was distantly aware of their children milling around them, of the fragrance of birch burning in the fireplace and other guests talking quietly. But all he could see were Colleen's magic-making eyes, the square set of her small shoulders under the big coat, her slender hands, one on Angel's head, one on Claudie's shoulder.

It was a nice picture.

Then that flirty Cassandra Somebody, who'd stopped him in the parking area, breezed past with her aunts and created a stir of expensive couture and musky scent.

She looked at him over her shoulder and said quietly, "I'll see you at breakfast."

His attention had been focused on Colleen and the unexpected power of her smile, and Mike had difficulty concentrating on what Cassandra was saying.

"Breakfast?" she prompted.

Breakfast. Yes. That was something he understood. "Yes," he said.

Cassandra smiled with what appeared to be deep satisfaction and followed her aunts to the desk.

When he turned back to Colleen, her smile had been replaced with an expression of cool politeness. "Thank you for driving my car back," she said. "And please don't feel any more responsibility toward it. Or us. Enjoy your stay. Boys?"

He wasn't sure he understood the change in her. The implication was that she hadn't liked him speaking to Cassandra, whom he'd never seen before today. But that implied Colleen felt something for him. He'd suspected she did, but he thought it was hatred.

He had to reassess, here.

"I just asked the boys," he said, "if they'd join the girls and me for Chinese checkers in our room."

"It's late," she said frostily.

"It's eight-thirty," he insisted.

"Bugsy's only four."

"You're on vacation."

"Mo-om!" Bill pleaded quietly.

"I'm almost five!" Bugsy argued.

She knew it was ridiculous, but she stopped to counter that claim. "Honey, your birthday isn't until October. That's…" She started to count.

"Seven and a half months if you count the rest of this one," Claudie said. To Bugsy, she added, "So you're not really even four and a half." Then, realizing that in her determination to clarify things, she'd undermined her father's purpose, she added lamely, "But you can nap on the bed if you get tired."

Made to feel like a baby, Bugsy started to cry.

Angel punched her sister.

"You should just mind your own business!" Bill snapped at Claudie. He usually loathed the ground Bugsy walked on and lived to cause him grief—until someone else tried to hurt him.

Claudie squared her stance, looking indignant. "I was just trying to help your mom…"

"Well, you should have just butted out!" Bill took Bugsy's hand. "I'll take him upstairs, Mom."

Mike gave Claudie their key. "You guys want to go upstairs, too? I'll be right behind you."

"I didn't mean to hurt his feelings," Claudie said glumly.

"I know you didn't." Colleen leaned down to hug her. "He's just kind of sensitive, being the youngest."

"Everybody thinks you're a baby," Angel complained. "I used to be four. It's bad."

Colleen nodded empathetically.

The girls ran upstairs. The moment they were out of earshot, Mike caught Colleen's arm and drew her through the living room, into the sunporch.

"Good work, Miss Arctic Circle," he said, squaring off against her in the middle of the room. It had begun to rain again, and the musical rhythm against the windows was completely at odds with the mood inside. "What is your problem, anyway? Seems to me we've both agreed the accidents today, although partly my fault, were not deliberate. I'm trying to do my best to make things right, but all you're doing is making things difficult. Are you always such a pill or is it the special circumstances?''

He was horrified when her eyes brimmed with tears. Then she shook them off with a toss of her head and said in a tight, high voice, "I'm sorry. I was excited about this trip and it's been one disaster after another, and this was just our first day here! So you'll pardon me if I'm less than cordial. I have no collision insurance, but I'm going to have to find a way to replace the door. I'm already paying my mechanic one hundred dollars a month, which I can't afford, for the alternator he replaced in December."

He opened his mouth to speak, but she cut him off with a finger pointed at him and a sharply spoken, "And don't you *dare* offer to take care of it for me— even if you're going to offer to let me pay you back. That doesn't solve anything. Money to him or money to you doesn't make any difference."

He understood her plight. Money had been tight when he was in school, then in the early days of his career when he'd had to support an office, a staff and a home. Marianne had complained there was never enough, even after his practice became lucrative.

"Doesn't your husband help?" he asked calmly.

He could see in her eyes that she had a lot to say about that, but she finally replied with a simple "No. He doesn't."

"You're divorced?"

"Yes."

"So am I."

She nodded. "Claudie told me. Your wife was cranky because she thought you never had enough money. Well, my husband couldn't have cared less about money. Which, generally, is an attitude I could endorse if I didn't have children who should eat regularly, wear clothes and have a roof over their heads—and if it wasn't so impractical to drive a car without a door."

"I'm sorry."

"Thank you, but it's not your problem." She gave him a look that was determined to keep him at a distance, then tried to walk around him. "Good night, Mike."

He knew this was going to get him into trouble, but there was a certain excitement to fighting with her that made him willing to live on the edge. He caught her arm and held her in place.

"What if I took care of it and you *didn't* have to pay me back?" he proposed.

She gave him just the suspicious, knowing look he expected.

"No," he assured her, "you don't have to sleep with me, either."

There was a subtle change in her expression—less knowing, more confused.

"You don't have to do *anything*," he clarified. "I appreciate the spot you're in, it was partly my fault, and I'd like to help. That's all."

Her mouth reshaped itself three times as she tried

to reply, then she finally shook her head. "You've known me all of four hours."

"Is there a time requirement on the offer of friend-ship?"

"If it's going to cost you four figures, there should be."

"No. There shouldn't."

She was stunned.

He was fascinated by that. It was interesting to ob-serve a woman with such a quick mouth suddenly speechless. He could see in her eyes that she was reassessing her opinion of him. He detected interest there, a little eagerness even, and he could have sworn her body made the smallest move toward him.

Then every positive inclination in her was extin-guished like a light and she said quietly, "Thank you, but no. It's very kind of you, but I would feel in-debted and that's just…dangerous ground."

He tipped his head back impatiently. "I promised there'd be no strings. Do you need an oath?"

"No." She put a hand to his arm in emphasis, and the sensation ricocheted crazily inside him until he was momentarily disoriented.

She withdrew her hand quickly, apparently expe-riencing the same response. The magic was there in her eyes, but this time she wasn't making it.

"No," she replied again, her voice breathless. She cleared her throat and squared her shoulders. "I'm finally in charge of my life and I like that. I don't have much, but I don't owe anybody, either."

"But you'd owe me only kindness," he reminded her. "Not money."

She smiled a little grimly. "Even that's a debt. Thank you for your help, but I'll take it from here."

She tried to walk away again, but he held her gently in place. "Divorce shouldn't make you fearful," he said. "Otherwise, fear becomes your only identity."

"I'm not fearful!" she insisted. "I'm free and I want to stay that way."

It was on the tip of his tongue to say that he was offering only the services of a good auto body shop, until he saw the awareness in her eyes. She liked him. He was now sure of it. It was an adolescent observation, he realized, and he reacted to it with a sudden excitement appropriate to adolescence.

She didn't want anything to do with him because she found him interesting and she was determined to steer clear of involvement.

This morning, he'd been certain he wanted to steer clear of romance, too. Now he wasn't so sure.

He spread both arms in a gesture of defeat and pretended to back off. "Okay, then. Enjoy your stay. We'll keep out of your way."

She looked first grateful, then disappointed, then grateful again. "Thank you," she replied. "We'll do the same."

She extended her hand, then must have remembered the previous moment of contact and thought better of it. Putting her hand behind her back, she said, "Good night, Mike," and hurried away.

He watched her go, thinking she was probably right and the most prudent thing to do was to keep a safe distance from each other. But he'd been self-protective since Marianne left, and frankly he was tired of it. It prevented him from getting hurt again, but it was also boring.

He made a decision on the spot. He was going to pursue Colleen O'Connor.

There. He always felt better when he had a plan in place.

CHAPTER FOUR

COLLEEN AND THE BOYS ate the last of their breakfast on the sunporch the following morning while Chuie munched her beef and liver. The cat had slept all night on Colleen's chest, though Colleen had slept only fitfully.

She'd worried about the car, she'd worried about the money to fix the car, she'd worried about the man who'd offered to have the car fixed for her. And, for reasons she couldn't understand, she'd worried about never running into him again.

But that was stupid and female, she told herself firmly as she helped Bugsy peel his orange. She couldn't afford to indulge her latent sexual fantasies. She had two boys to care for and support and there simply wasn't time or effort left over for…for…

She was mentally struggling with her own argument when she looked across the back lawn and saw the subject of her thoughts walking with the large Saint Bernard on a leash, the girls scampering ahead of him. They hadn't been at the breakfast table when she and the boys had come down, and she'd overheard the elegant smoothie asking Maureen where he was.

"He and his daughters took off early with the dog," Maureen had replied. "They'll be having breakfast when they come back."

The smoothie had sighed. "Just my luck. We have to leave for our meeting in ten minutes."

"I'm sorry," Maureen said.

Colleen had heard the underlying lack of sincerity in the innkeeper's tone. Apparently Maureen didn't like the woman, either.

As Colleen watched the Flynns, Claudie raced back toward her father with something held up for him to look at. He leaned over it, nodded. Angel came back to them to wrap her arms around the dog, the dog leapt playfully at her, and the two fell to the ground. Claudie jumped on top and Mike joined in the fray. Through the checkerboard of small-paned windows, Colleen could hear laughter and barking.

"They sure have a lot of fun, don't they," Bill observed wistfully, moving closer to the glass to watch them.

The pang in his voice ripped open a wound in Colleen's heart.

"*We* have a lot of fun," she said.

He continued to watch them. "Yeah, but it's girl fun."

Girl fun? "What do you mean?"

"When you get paid, we go to the movies, you take us skating, we have picnics in the summer. But we never roll around in the grass. We don't have a dog or play football in the park.''

''Because I don't know how to play football.''

'''Cause you're a girl.''

''I'm your mother. I'm supposed to be a girl.''

Bill smiled at her over his shoulder, the gesture accepting her as beloved even though she stood in the way of him having guy fun.

Colleen sipped her tea. She and the boys had relished every bite of the breakfast buffet. At home she usually just had cereal or toast because it was nutritious and inexpensive, and she didn't have time for fancy preparations. This morning they'd enjoyed eggs and bacon and wonderful griddle cakes with real maple syrup that were Clint Cooper's specialty. She was determined to leave here with pleasant memories, even if they were just of the food.

She hadn't been out to look at her car yet and didn't intend to. It was an easy walk to town, and she and the boys would spend the day exploring. There was no point worrying about the car until it was time to go back to New Bedford. Then she'd find a way to rig something over the door to keep the boys warm and safe until she got home to the trusted mechanic who would extend her credit.

Colleen heard the commotion in the dining room as the Flynns joined the other guests for breakfast.

''You just missed Cassandra,'' she heard Maureen say.

Mike gave a quiet reply that Colleen couldn't make out.

Impatient with herself, she gathered up the boys' plates and cups and carried them with hers into the kitchen, which could be reached without going into the dining room. She found a tea bag, filled her cup with more hot water, and was wandering back to the sunporch just as Maureen walked into the kitchen with an empty fruit plate.

"The Flynns are eating," she said, implying that Colleen join them. With a grin she added, "And Mike took the dog upstairs, so you're safe."

"Thanks," Colleen replied, "but as soon as I've had my second cup of tea, the boys and I are going to town."

"Hi, Colleen!" Claudie appeared behind Maureen. She wore bright yellow pants and a turtleneck top embroidered with gold stars. Her hair was tied back with a pair of barrettes too small to hold the thick, glossy mass. "After breakfast, can you do my hair?" she asked with a roll of her eyes. "Dad's no good at it and I can't find my big barrettes."

"Um...sure." Colleen couldn't deny the child's request just because she had difficulty with her father.

Claudie looked relieved. "Thanks. Angel could use help, too."

"Okay. The boys and I are on the sunporch when you're finished with breakfast. And don't rush."

Claudie skipped away.

"Cute little girls," Maureen observed.

"Yes." Colleen headed back toward the porch. "They're adorable."

"He likes your boys."

Colleen turned to look at Maureen. Hearing praise for her children always brightened her mood.

"Who does?"

"Mike. He said Bill was a character and Bugsy a sweet little boy."

He was right on target. She wondered how he'd had time to analyze them when she felt as though he'd spent every moment picking on her. But she liked the fact that he liked them.

She took a sip of her tea and asked with a smile, "Are you matchmaking, Maureen?"

Maureen's eyes widened innocently. "I don't have time for that. I'm just trying to keep all my guests happy."

Colleen saw through that excuse. "Because it occurs to me that he'd be perfect for you."

Maureen laughed lightly. "I'm too busy to tend to a husband. He'd have to be able to take care of himself. Like an air fern."

A boy walked into the kitchen, a bag of groceries in his arms. He was taller than Colleen, but she guessed him to be a young teen. He bore a resemblance to Maureen.

"Here you go," he said, putting the bag on the counter. "More bananas, and a quart of whipping cream. Tell me you're making penuche with…the…

cream.'' His words slowed as he caught sight of Colleen.

''Colleen, this is my nephew, Keegan,'' Maureen said, putting an arm around the boy, who was watching Colleen with a serious stare. ''Keegan, this is Mrs. O'Connor. She and her boys are staying with us for a week.''

''Hi!'' Colleen came forward to shake his hand. ''It's nice to meet you, Keegan.''

He had a good grip, she noted. And clear green eyes that seemed to be studying her with purpose. ''You're married?'' he asked in concern.

Maureen rolled her eyes. ''Keegan…''

He turned to her with a quieting gesture of his hand. ''Don't get upset, Aunt Maureen. I'm just asking.''

Colleen raised an eyebrow. ''Are you wife-hunting?'' she teased. ''At…what? Thirteen?''

''Twelve,'' he replied. He had a youthful charm about him, yet an impressively adult ease with a stranger. ''And yes. But not for me.''

Maureen patted his shoulder. ''He wants to marry his father off. Thinks he needs female companionship.''

Keegan elbowed her gently. ''You wouldn't have to do his laundry anymore.''

''Yeah,'' Maureen agreed grimly, ''and he'd probably stop cooking for me and start cooking for *her*. I think he's fine being single.''

''He's six-three,'' Keegan said, clearly determined

to put his father's best features forward. "He's a scratch golfer, he hunts only with a camera, and he can out-bench-press anybody! He's smart, funny, he drew up the plans to remodel this whole place and did a lot of the work himself."

"I've met him and he's charming," Colleen assured him, "and he sounds like the perfect husband for someone. Unfortunately, I'm really happy being single."

Keegan seemed able to accept that. "Right. Lots of people say that until they meet the right person, then…" He made an explosive sound, his arms spreading out to indicate the blast. "They're in love."

Maureen handed him a banana. "I don't think people like to think of love in terms of blowing things up."

Keegan gave his aunt a comically disapproving look. "An emotional explosion, Aunt Maureen."

Maureen smiled at her guest. "This boy's just too smart for his own good. Keegan, Colleen's out of the running as a wife for your father, okay?"

"There's a very beautiful woman named Cassandra staying here," Colleen said. "She came in last night and seems to be on the lookout for a man."

Keegan made a face. "Not his type."

"Shouldn't he decide that?"

"He did. She tried to come on to him this morning when we were replacing the bulb in the upstairs hallway. She pretended to trip and he got down off the ladder to help her up.'' He mimicked a helpless feminine gesture by placing the back of his wrist to his forehead. ''It was so phony. She held on to him for a long time and he practically had to peel her off him to help her limp to that chair near the stairs. Then Dad got a call, her aunt told her to hurry up, that they'd be late for their meeting, and I saw her run down the stairs without limping at all.''

Maureen pulled apart the bunch of bananas and placed them in the empty fruit bowl. ''A vamp in our midst,'' she said, reaching into the refrigerator for three oranges. ''She's after Mike Flynn, too.''

''You might change your mind about my dad,'' Keegan suggested as Maureen added the oranges and a bunch of red grapes to the bowl, then handed it to Keegan. ''When you get to know him, that is. Is Mike Flynn the guy with the Saint Bernard?''

''Right.''

''He's cool. He gave me five bucks to get him a *Wall Street Journal* when I went for your groceries.'' He took the paper out of the bag and smiled from his aunt to Colleen. ''But he's got two little girls and all my dad has is me. I'm very low maintenance— which is more than you can say for little girls. Nice to meet you, Mrs. O'Connor.''

''My pleasure, Keegan. And you can call me Colleen.''

He went off with a wave of the newspaper.

''He's so in tune with his world, he's scary,'' Colleen said with a laugh.

Maureen nodded. "Just like his father. You might want to give Clint some consideration. He's just the kind of man today's woman is looking for—all man but as sweet as they come."

"Thanks, but men in general are what I'm trying to avoid, sweet or not. By the way, breakfast was wonderful."

Claudie and Angel were already waiting for her on the sunporch, their father sitting on the floor with Bill, talking Red Sox statistics. Bugsy sat on the other side of Mike, his elbow resting on the man's knee, his complete attention focused on Mike, though she was sure he didn't understand a word.

Mike stood when she walked in. "Good morning," he said with restrained courtesy. "Claudie claims you said you'd do their hair?" He appeared apologetic. "If you were bullied into this…"

She shook her head before he could finish. "Not at all. I don't get much chance to do hair with the boys." She indicated the very short style Bill, and therefore Bugsy, preferred.

"You're sure?"

"Yes."

"All right, then. Would you mind if the boys and I shoot hoops in the parking lot while you girls *do hair?*" He made a face over the last two words that caused the boys to giggle.

"Not at all." The boys raced instantly toward the door, excited beyond words. "Wait!" she called. "You have to get your coats, and you have to promise me you'll be polite and stay right with Mr. Flynn.''

They promised. Of course, she knew they'd have promised to eat spinach for a week if it meant they got to go have some ''guy fun.''

She was spared hurt feelings because the girls seemed equally excited to be with her. While she French-braided their hair, they talked about clothes, makeup and Britney Spears.

''HOW COME YOU LIVE IN BOSTON?'' Bugsy asked as Mike held him up to the basket for a shot. ''We live in New Bedford.''

'''Cause I was born in Boston,'' Mike replied, lining the boy up. ''And I really like it there. Easy. Take your time. Stay really steady, then let out your breath when you shoot. There!''

''But I missed!''

''But you got really close. Bill's turn.''

Mike swung Bugsy to the ground, then stood back while Bill dribbled fairly skillfully, then leapt at the basket and missed.

''Damn it!'' Bill said.

''Hey.'' Mike frowned at him as Bill tossed him the ball. ''Your mom lets you say *damn*?''

Bill admitted honestly, ''No. But she doesn't know how to have guy fun, either.''

''Well, guy fun doesn't have to involve talking bad or acting stupid.'' He tossed him back the ball. ''Shoot that same way but put a little more into your jump. You'd have sunk it if you'd been a little taller, or there'd been more arc to the ball.''

This time he almost made it, but it bounced off the rim. Mike gave him another shot.

''Isn't it our turn?'' Bugsy asked.

Mike nodded. ''Bill's almost got it. We have to give him a little time. Come on, Bill. Third time's a charm.''

Bill dribbled the ball, focused on the basket, leapt with great concentration and dunked the ball as though Michael Jordan had helped. He jumped up and down in excitement.

''Our dad lives in Bermuda,'' Bugsy said as Bill, generous in success, tossed the ball gently at him. ''He forgot Bill's birthday. Mom was mad.''

Mike put Bugsy onto his shoulders and placed himself just in front of the basket. ''The world is full of people who forget other people are important. Even some parents are like that.''

''Mom cried.''

''When you're selfish, the thoughtless things you do hurt other people. And it looks like you get away with it because you're not the one getting hurt. But someday it catches up with you.''

''How?'' Bill asked.

Mike waited while Bugsy made his shot. He sunk it and pounded gleefully on Mike's head. Mike began to wonder if this was really a good idea.

''The world's a give-and-take kind of place,'' he replied to Bill, moving back slightly so that Bugsy could take another shot. "If you're going to take kindness from people and let them do things for you without returning their favors and helping them back, word's going to get around. Pretty soon you won't have any friends. And if you don't have friends, then you're not part of things and you're pretty much alone."

"I don't like to be alone," Bugsy said. "When we're bad and we have time-outs, we have to sit alone in our room. I get lonesome. The clock gets scary."

Bill shook his head at his brother. "It's a Bugs Bunny clock," he said in disbelief. "How can you be afraid of a Bugs Bunny clock?"

Bugsy leaned away from Mike's shoulder to reply aggressively, "'Cause it gets loud, okay!"

Mike clamped his hands over the boy's knees. "Bugs. You're supposed to be concentrating on the shot."

"Well, he's always laughing at me."

"I'm not laughing," Bill said, a smirk belying his words. "I just think it's funny that somebody could be afraid of a Bugs Bunny clock."

"Even familiar noises can be scary when you're alone," Mike said, lining Bugsy up to the basket a little farther away than he'd been for the last shot. "Are you concentrating, Bugs?"

"Yeah."

Mike felt the inclination of the boy's little body

as he pitched forward to throw the ball. It sank again and he squealed his delight.

"When do you have to go home?" Bill asked after a few more baskets.

"Next Sunday morning," Mike replied.

Bill took his stance and aimed at the basket. "I wish we could stay till Sunday, but Mom says we have to go home Saturday so we have Sunday to do laundry and get ready for Monday. She always has to organize everything."

"Yeah, well, if things aren't organized they tend to fall apart."

"But you're going Sunday."

"That's because the girls' mom does their laundry and gets things organized. I don't have to do that." He wanted to change that, though. He was gathering his arguments and planned to confront Marianne with them when she returned.

"How far away is Boston from New Bedford?" Bill seemed to completely forget the basket and tossed the ball absently in his hands as they talked. Bugsy, still on Mike's shoulders, held on to Mike's ears and hummed.

"About fifty miles."

"My class went there once to see the Boston Tea Party Ship. We got to throw tea chests into the water."

"Yeah, those are neat places."

"New Bedford used to have a lot of guys who fished for whales."

"Yes."

"You don't use a pole, you know. You have this spear kind of thing."

"A harpoon."

"Yeah. And guys go out in little boats to get around the whale." Bill looked grim. "I'd be scared."

"I imagine they were."

"I bet the whale was, too. I couldn't kill anything, even if I needed the oil for my lamp. They didn't have light bulbs then."

"Right." Mike kept his smile to himself.

"Claudie's very smart." Bill suddenly turned, gauged his distance from the basket, leapt gracefully and sank the shot.

"Yes, she is," Mike agreed, and wondered if the point of this conversation was that Claudie wasn't the only one with brains.

Colleen and the girls came outside. The girls were wearing their coats, and their hair was tamed into neat braids. They were beaming.

"Daddy, Colleen's going to town, too," Claudie said excitedly. "Can't we all go together?"

Colleen looked trapped. He tried to give her an out. "They may want to see different things than we—"

"We were just gonna check out the Minuteman in the park," Bill said eagerly, "and probably just do boring stuff like look at old buildings and find little shops and someplace to eat. Huh, Mom?"

"Yes, that's about right," she answered. Mike saw that she was trying to read his mind. Did he want her to go with them? Did he not? She wasn't sure what to make of the fact that he'd backed off in getting to know her. This was good.

"Or, if Colleen has other plans," he suggested, "we can take Bill and Bugs with us, and she can…"

"Can we, Mom?" Bill demanded before the words were even out of his mouth.

COLLEEN KNEW BETTER than to suffer hurt feelings over her children's eagerness to spend time with other people. That meant they were adjusting well socially, not that they would be just as happy without her.

But she felt vaguely wounded, anyway. The boys were clearly bonding with this man. She'd watched them from the window while she was braiding the girls' hair. They were animated and talkative. Mike Flynn was tall and strong and they'd been without a father for two years. They appreciated the security he represented.

But he wasn't theirs and they would have to understand that.

Still, a lively wind had blown away the rain, the sun shone brightly and the air was crisp and perfumed. She couldn't force reality on anyone today. This was a day made for play and dreams.

"Colleen, please come!" Claudie begged, holding on to her hand. "Please, please, please!"

Angel held her other hand and tried to tug her toward the car. "Come on!" she ordered. "Come on, Colleen!"

"Okay," she said finally, then met Mike's gaze. "If you're sure we're not intruding on a family day."

"Not at all," he assured her. "I'll get Chewie." Then he winced. "Is your Chuie going to want to come?"

She had to laugh. "She's asleep on a pillow on the hearth. Maureen said it was all right to leave her there." She gathered up the children. "And while the dog's being rounded up, we can all make a bathroom stop."

The children groaned at her but complied.

COOPER'S CORNER WAS FILLED with the little stores Bill insisted his mother would look for. Antique shops abounded, along with those selling colonial memorabilia, Americana, and all kinds of gifts and trinkets.

Colleen had given the boys a little money to spend, and the girls had gone back up to their rooms for their purses before they left. Mike and Colleen waited patiently in a bead shop while the girls pored over hundreds of tiny bins filled with beads of all sizes.

The boys were fascinated with leather thongs and Native American beads on the other side of the shop.

Mike and Colleen waited by a rack of craft books

somewhere in the middle. Colleen picked one out and flipped through it.

"I've always wanted to try to do punch tin," she said with a sigh. "The instructions often say you can do it with a nail and hammer, but that isn't true. I tried it."

"There must be tools for it," Mike suggested helpfully.

"There are. Once I get my car door replaced, I might try it." She realized how that sounded and looked up from the book, quickly apologetic. "That wasn't intended as a jab at you or a whine. I was just talking."

He raised an eyebrow. "I didn't take it personally."

He did have the most interesting eyes—darker blue than she'd ever seen before. And when they looked at her, she got the impression they could see everything in her pockets—physical and emotional.

"Good." She shifted her weight and flipped a page in the magazine without looking at it. "Our children seem determined to get to know one another. That's going to force us to get along."

"Is that the only reason you want to?" he asked.

She looked him in the eye. "Now *you're* jabbing."

"Sorry. I just wondered."

Claudie came to him with a palmful of beads, which he leaned down to admire. Then she turned to show Colleen. When the girl went to the counter with them, Colleen said quietly, "I just meant that there'd really be no reason for your life and mine to intersect if it wasn't for the children."

He fixed her with that look. She knew without a doubt that he saw her interest in him, somehow knew it had kept her awake part of the night, knew it raised the tension level in her even now.

"Pants on fire, Mrs. O'Connor," he whispered to her as Bugsy ran to her with a knife-scabbard kit that included complicated beading.

She had to shake off Mike's rumbling, scolding voice to concentrate on her son. "I think that's too complicated for you, Bugs," she said. "I'll come and help you find something easier."

"But I want this one!" he said in a pout, and walked dejectedly back to where he'd found it.

"I believe what I said," she whispered back to Mike as Angel approached, needing fifty cents more. He gave it to her.

"No, you don't," he challenged. "You're afraid to make a move toward me because you think you wouldn't have time to handle a relationship if one developed, which is sad but understandable. Or else you're afraid you've lost the skill required to attract and hold a partner so you don't even want to try, which is sad and cowardly."

She gasped in indignation.

He shrugged. "Sorry. I know that's bold on such short acquaintance, but getting to know you is important to me."

"Even though you think I haven't the skill to attract and hold a partner?" She emphasized his words.

"I didn't say I thought that," he corrected. "I said you did."

"You presume to know what's in my mind? My heart?"

"I have to presume. You won't show me."

"Mo-om!" In the corner, Bugs held up a colorful plastic envelope. "This one?"

She was trembling with exasperation. Afraid of what she might do to Mike Flynn if she stood near him another moment, she went to Bugsy.

It was another half hour before everyone made their choices, changed their minds, finally made their purchases, then left the shop.

They toured a small local museum filled with Native American artifacts, Revolutionary memorabilia and photos of Cooper's Corner from its inception to the present. The boys went with Mike to look at an old fire truck, and the girls followed Colleen to study the beading on a buckskin dress.

They had lunch afterward, the children talking incessantly about all they'd seen, then squabbling over who'd made the best purchase at the bead shop. It was hardly necessary for Mike and Colleen to speak at all. Which was a good thing, because though Colleen was no longer seething, she was now confused. And that always made her grumpy.

The control she held on her life often felt so tenuous that she tended to panic if she stopped to think about it. So she didn't think about it. That way she maintained control by the simple act of forward propulsion. She didn't stop to examine what was missing, what she wanted and didn't have, what it meant in the overall scheme of things.

She had the most awful feeling that if she stopped to consider whether or not to let Mike Flynn into her life, even just a little way, everything would fall apart on her.

She was beginning to see that this was her biggest problem with him. His appeal tended to confuse her, shake her sense of having control over things, make her crabby.

Well, she had a thing or two to show him. He'd suggested she was chicken. He was going to have to pay for that.

After lunch, they went to the village green and checked out the statue of the Minuteman. The plaque read, "In honor of the men of Massachusetts who died so that we may live in freedom."

Their interest piqued in local history, they walked over to the library, where they looked up information on Theodore Cooper, the town's founder. They discovered that he and his descendants had farmed in the area, enduring harsh winters and hard times. Besides being successful farmers, the Coopers were known for producing a set of twins each generation, and the pairs of oaks that lined the drive up to the bed-and-breakfast were in their honor.

It was late afternoon when Mike, Colleen and the children finally went back to Twin Oaks.

Maureen was sweeping the steps and the children ran to her, elbowing one another out of the way, to show off their purchases.

Before Mike could follow them, Colleen caught his arm and yanked him around to face her, determined that he would pay for his unfair judgment of her character. "Hey!" she said.

His expression was half amused, half intrigued. "Yes?"

"Sunporch," she commanded. "Nine o'clock tonight. Be there." Then she hurried off to join the children.

CHAPTER FIVE

MIKE GUESSED HE WAS IN for another chewing out as he made his way to the sunporch. Not that the prospect upset him. Living with Marianne had hardened him against arguments where he was continually judged to be the one at fault. He volunteered too often for the medical teams that went to Mexico on humanitarian missions, she'd said. He did too much pro bono work. He wasn't sufficiently dedicated to the money track their friends were on and the lifestyle it led to.

At least Colleen's complaints would have a different tone. He had been painfully honest with her today, but it was hard to deal with the protective shield she kept around her day in and day out. He'd thought she'd finally dispensed with it this morning, only to discover in the bead shop that it was still in place. Their lives need only intersect because of their children, she'd said. Ha!

And then he'd forgotten that he'd intended to keep his distance, to keep her guessing, to try to pique her curiosity. He'd been aware only that she smelled like flowers but showed him thorns.

Maureen had asked the girls and Colleen's boys to help her make paper cutouts of shamrocks and hats for a St. Patrick's Day event coming up at the end of the week, and Chewie was stretched out in front of the fire in the gathering room, enjoying the attention of a couple of guests who were fascinated by his sweetness and his size.

Mike passed through the gathering room and turned the corner to the sunporch, a little surprised to find it in darkness. He reached for the light switch, but a soft, small hand came down on his with surprising power, stopping the action. He caught the scent of flowers.

Two hands took a firm hold of his arm and pushed him deeper into the room, away from the door. He didn't resist. This was too promising.

"Why, Mrs. O'Connor, you..." he began as he found himself in the dark corner between the wicker sofa and a bookshelf. But his words were cut off by a hand over his mouth.

"Don't speak!" Colleen whispered. "You've accused me of being a matronly coward and it's my turn to rebut."

"I didn't..." he mumbled, intending to remind her that he hadn't accused her of such behavior, just suggested she might think that of herself. But he was rendered silent again by the pressure of her soft flesh.

It wasn't her hand this time, but her lips.

While the fragrant darkness pulsed around him and quiet laughter drifted from the gathering room, Colleen caught his face in her hands and kissed him with formidable passion.

Surprise held him paralyzed, and she used it to her advantage. Her lips explored his, nudged and nipped at them until they parted, then she eased the tip of an exploring tongue inside.

At the same time, she thrust her fingers into his hair, causing a ripple of sensation along his scalp and down his spine. Her hands followed the line of his neck and across his shoulders, and might have continued down his back except that she didn't seem able to reach. They massaged down his arms instead, then up again, one fingertip exploring the rim of his ear and tracing inside.

Every nerve ending in his body was alive and quivering.

Her kiss set off a powerful sensation deep inside him, and the calm with which he'd handled his sexless life all this time was smashed to smithereens.

She nipped at his bottom lip once more, then dropped her hands to his shoulders, as though holding him in place.

Keeping her voice low, she said, "You supermale types think that if a woman doesn't react to you, it's because she lacks desire. It seems to escape you that she could be as hot as you are, but simply discerning or not attracted to you. So there. Remember that kiss and try to tell yourself I'm a coward."

She dropped her hands from him, the blissful moment suddenly and abruptly over. Or so she thought.

He saw her pale eyes in the shadows as she gave him one last judicious look, then turned away.

Reaching out blindly in the dark, he caught a fistful of her sweater and pulled her back to him.

"I obviously mean something to you," he said softly, wrapping his arms around her as she tried to wriggle away, "or that kiss wouldn't have had such impact."

She looked momentarily at a loss, then tossed her head haughtily. "I'm just more skilled than you give me credit for."

"You are skilled," he granted her, "but your heartbeat's slamming against my chest. Don't tell me that kiss meant nothing to you except proof of your prowess."

"It meant there's chemistry," she admitted after a moment. "Nothing else."

"If that was simply chemistry," he argued, "it was *nuclear* chemistry. Why are you trembling if it meant nothing?" He was going to make her admit she felt something for him if he had to keep her here all night.

OKAY, COLLEEN, NOT ONE of your best ideas, she told herself as she stood wrapped in Mike's arms, her heart apparently prepared to beat its way out of her chest. She and Danny had had very little sexual contact their last year together. They'd hardly even kissed, except for a perfunctory gesture on some holiday or other. And there'd been no time for men since. She'd obviously forgotten that a kiss could make you feel as though it had changed your molecular structure.

She tried to catch her breath, quiet her pulse, stop the trembling. "I'm shaking," she whispered, "because the sunporch is cold."

"You're wearing a thick sweater."

"I feel cold inside," she fibbed, "because you called me a coward."

He laughed then, and cupping her head in his hand, tipped it back so he could look into her eyes. "I don't believe that, but if it's true, you certainly proved me wrong, didn't you?"

"I did?"

"You did. Takes a lot of guts to prove to a man that you have that much passion, that much depth. Particularly one you're trying to discourage. You must have known that kiss would make me even more determined to spend time with you."

Well, her scheme had backfired big time. "Mike," she said reasonably, "you're not getting the point here."

He shook his head. "You're the one missing it. Somewhere inside you—maybe even subconsciously—you want me to know how you feel. You just don't want to have to say the words because then you'd have to admit it to yourself."

She considered his words a moment, then said with a frown, "I think you perceive me as more complex than I really am. I usually have little trouble saying what I feel. Surely you've noticed that?"

"No, I think you're comfortable saying what you think, but not necessarily what you feel. Subtle but significant difference. And anyway, you're not the only one in this. You want to know how I feel?"

Oh, God. She was going to regret this. She just knew she was.

"Can you be brief?" she asked.

"I don't think so," he replied frankly, then went on to communicate his feelings.

He lowered his head slowly, tortured her with anticipation, then put his lips to hers with a tenderness that was almost more exciting than passion. He was communicating something else entirely, and she found herself straining closer so that she didn't miss it.

I could come on strong, his gentle, artful caresses said. *I have the skill and the experience. But I'm trying to tell you that this is for you. That you can deny me all you want, but you'll find yourself turning to me because you need comfort and kindness.*

The touch of his hands was a delicious counterpoint to the tender message. She felt the restrained strength in them as they roved her back and bracketed her small waist, one hand exploring lower to shape the curve of her hip.

Though she'd loved Danny in the first few years of their marriage, she couldn't recall that he'd ever touched her with the intention of pleasing her. His own pleasure had always been his goal, and if she'd enjoyed the exercise, all the better for both of them.

This focus on her was a totally new experience. And somehow it made her feel stronger rather than weaker. But it also created a sense of trust in her that surprised her. She let herself succumb to Mike's superior strength and leaned on him in the conviction that she was safe.

His arms tightened around her, and since escape was the last thing on her mind, she simply snuggled closer and expelled a breath of acceptance.

The light filled the sunporch with sudden, blinding brilliance. Maureen stood in the doorway, a hand over her mouth, her eyes wide with apology. Beside her stood a large man, probably as tall as Mike but twice his size. He was bald, wore glasses...and a Roman collar. Had Colleen been able to crawl inside Mike's pocket and disappear, she'd have happily done so.

She heard Mike's soft laughter, felt his comforting squeeze.

"I'm *so* sorry!" Maureen gasped. "I should have realized when I saw you heading in this direction that you might be...that you two..."

"It's all right." Mike caught Colleen's hand and drew her with him toward Maureen and the priest. Colleen would have happily stayed behind, but his grip was strong. He offered his free hand to the priest. "Good evening, Father," he said politely. "I'm Michael Flynn. This is Colleen O'Connor."

The priest's blue eyes twinkled as he shook Mike's hand, then Colleen's. "Maureen said she had a couple of Irish folk for me to meet, but I hadn't realized you'd be so blatantly Irish. Flynn and O'Connor, and with a passion for canoodling! I'm Jim Gallagher. I understand it's your brilliant children who are helping in the kitchen with the decorations for our St. Patrick's Day dance.''

Mike nodded. "The girls are mine. I didn't realize what the decorations were for—just trusted Maureen that they wouldn't be put to any illegal purpose." He cast her a teasing glance and she laughed.

"And the handsome boys are yours?" the priest asked Colleen. She cleared her throat, hoping she had a voice.

"Yes, Father. Bill and Bugsy. Well…his real name is Justin."

The priest nodded, then frowned. "Bugsy. Not named after Bugsy Malone, I trust. One of our Irish brethren, though not a credit to us."

Colleen smiled at his joke about the famous mobster. "No, Father. He's nicknamed after Bugs Bunny because he loves him so much. And I appreciate it because it makes him eat his carrots."

Now the priest laughed. "Smart woman. I understand you're in the greeting card business."

Surprised that he knew that, Colleen nodded. "Yes, sort of. I mean, I'm actually a checker in a supermarket. But I freelance with verses to supplement our income."

"Perfect. I need someone to write a verse that'll welcome guests to our dinner and dance. St. Bridget's is filled with wonderful people working hard on the project, but no one seems to be able to come up with just the right thing. When I stopped by tonight to check on decorations and told Maureen my plight, she suggested you right away.''

"Oh, Father." Colleen made a face. "It's been weeks since I've felt even a glimmer of creativity. Life's been a little…challenging lately, and I think whatever skill I had has sort of…you know…dried up."

He smiled. "When Maureen and I walked in here, it seemed as though other skills were quite fruitful. The Good Lord has created us so that when one skill blossoms, it can encourage life in another. Will you see what you can do?"

She found it difficult to resist such charming persistence. "When do you need this?"

"It should be on the door of the church by five-thirty Friday evening when our guests begin arriving for dinner. I think it would be most effective on parchment. Can you do calligraphy?"

"Calligraphy…uh, yes. A little."

"Good." He seemed pleased and shook her hand again, then Mike's. "If there's anything I can do for you, I hope you'll come and see me. The rectory is always open."

"Thank you, Father."

He nodded, then offered his arm to Maureen. "Good work, young lady. Can we see if there are any more of those cookies the children were eating?"

"Of course, Father." With another apologetic

glance at Mike and Colleen, Maureen drew the priest away.

Colleen walked toward the window and put both hands over her eyes. "I can't believe we were caught necking in a dark corner by a priest!"

She heard Mike's laughter. "He didn't seem offended. And we weren't necking—that's done for its own purpose. We were learning about each other. I learned that you do have guts, and you learned that I admire that in a woman."

She lowered her hands to find him standing behind her, a self-satisfied expression on his face.

If only she could blame him for what happened, but she couldn't. She was the one who had suggested the clandestine meeting, who had left the lights off in the clever plan that had backfired on her so completely.

With a groan, she sank into a chair. "Now I have to create a verse that will greet everyone in the parish and the priest as well."

"You'll think of something," he encouraged, sitting in the love seat opposite her. "Why didn't you tell me you write greeting cards?"

She leaned against the pillowed back and fixed him with a wry smile. "We've been too busy arguing. And what I told him is true. I haven't had a creative thought in my head in months. I have a great life, I'm not whining, but we live from paycheck to paycheck and something's always breaking down and one of the boys is always losing a jacket or a shoe. Bill's been argumentative about everything—I think because his father forgot his birthday. And though I've explained to him over and over that it's all right to love his father, he also has to accept that he's not a very giving human being, and I'm not sure you can expect an eight-year-old to understand that. Bugsy seems to be doing fine, but he's started crying when I drop him off at day care and I feel so guilty, but I have to go to work!''

Colleen heard herself talking, talking, talking. Even when she'd finally stopped, the words seemed to echo in the room. ''I claimed I wasn't whining,'' she grumbled in self-deprecation, ''then I went ahead and did it, anyway.''

''Telling someone your troubles isn't whining,'' Mike said gently. ''And who on earth made you feel you had to be Wonder Woman, anyway?''

She sighed, propped her feet on the matching hassock and stared at the ceiling fan. ''I guess I did it to myself. It's my nature. My mother died when Jerrianne and I were my children's ages. My father was basically good, but an alcoholic, so I became the mother. Jerri always introduces me to her friends as her sister, Mom.''

Mike took an afghan from the back of the love seat and placed it over her. Then he pulled off the spiffy leather booties she'd bought for half price at a bargain shoe shop.

''Keep talking,'' he said when she stopped.

''It's boring.''

"Not to me. I'm the guy who wants to learn more about you, remember?"

She grinned wickedly, feeling suddenly, inexplicably relaxed. "But I thought you were more interested in…physical things."

He resumed his seat and didn't smile. "Then you do me a disservice."

She felt chastened. "I'm sorry."

"It's okay. Go on."

"Well…" She tried to organize her thoughts on something she was just beginning to understand. "I think I know where I went wrong in my marriage. I mothered Danny instead of being a wife to him. I found solutions for all our problems, financial or otherwise. I tried to be understanding when he lost five jobs in one year. I listened to his excuses when he said he was going to the junior college for retraining in computers but was at the batting cages with his friends. It took me too long to get angry."

"You were being the adult," Mike said quietly, "and he used you. That's his fault as much as yours. You let it go on, but he did it in the first place."

"I just didn't want to admit it wasn't working."

"That's understandable. I did the same thing with Marianne."

"Why do we do that? It only makes us miserable longer."

"Got me. If I had an answer to that, I probably wouldn't have done it. I guess it's just hard to believe that you were wrong about what looked so right in the beginning. And now you have these children who are made up of the two of you and you can't simply walk away from it.''

She sat up, holding the afghan to her with her arms under it. ''That's exactly it. And you know if you break up you're going to have to stay connected because of the children, and that's going to complicate your life even more.'' She closed her eyes, remembering the day Danny told her he was leaving. She'd been so surprised to feel relief rather than dismay. ''Only you get to a point where you realize even that's got to be better than living with a stranger you no longer like, much less love.''

He nodded moodily. ''Absolutely.''

''And you swear you'll never take that chance again.''

''Yeah.''

That shared admission lingered in the air between them, a challenge to their kiss of moments ago.

She was too tired, too shaken to think very deeply about where this relationship might go—or even if it should get started.

''I think you just need input,'' Mike said briskly.

''Input?'' she repeated dumbly.

''To kick-start your creativity. We did everything the kids wanted today. Tomorrow, we should do whatever you need to help you relax and get your creative juices flowing. Walk in the woods, go to a movie…''

She settled more deeply into the afghan, an insidious languor stealing over her. "The boys will whine."

"Not if you explain. It's all right for them to know that you need things, too."

She smiled. "Kids don't usually get that. Well, little girls might, but little boys don't."

He frowned. "That's sexist and unfair. That's not an attitude you want to teach your children, is it? Your boys adore you. They'd do anything to make you happy. You should give them that chance."

That was all she remembered of the conversation. Her last thought was a little thrill at the prospect of another day in his company. It occurred to her she should be concerned about her growing attraction to him, but she was really too tired. That would have to wait for another day.

When she awoke, she was being placed in her bed, and Mike was leaning over her.

"What happened?" she asked groggily. "Where are the boys?" On the pillow beside her, Chuie opened her eyes, stretched out a paw, then went back to sleep.

"Here, Mom!" The boys clambered onto her bed, deeply amused.

"You fell asleep!" Bill said with what sounded like delight.

Claudie and Angel appeared on the other side of the bed, Chewie between them. The cat opened one watchful eye. "Daddy had to carry you up the stairs like you were a princess!"

She realized that letting herself feel embarrassed about that would only bring her to wakefulness and destroy the sweet wonder she felt at being in bed with Mike Flynn leaning over her.

Her brain wanted to spin out the possibilities, to imagine what would happen if she pulled him down to her. But they were surrounded by their children, and even though the scenario was unfolding only in her head, it had the potential to prompt real, live action.

"Thank you," she said simply, longing to touch him but sure it wasn't wise.

He seemed to read her thoughts. With reluctance in his eyes, he stood up straight and pointed to the boys' cots. "I'm going to trust you guys to brush your teeth and go to bed quietly so your mom doesn't have to get up, okay?"

Bill grinned. "I was going to sneak down to the kitchen for more cookies." At Mike's stern expression, he shook his head. "Just kidding. We'll brush our teeth and go to bed."

"Good. Tomorrow, your mom is planning our schedule and it would be nice if no one complained. She has some work to do for Father Gallagher and she needs to clear her mind."

"We're working for Father Gallagher, too!" Bugsy exclaimed. "He said we're going to be little leper— something." He turned questioningly to his brother. "What was it?"

"Leprechauns," Bill replied. "That's magic Irish

people. Maureen said we could help her all day tomorrow if we wanted to. Then Father says he could use our help at the church, 'cause lots of the kids who usually help have the flu.''

"Maureen said that?"

"Yeah, she was going to talk to you about it, but she said you and Mom were busy and she was going to wait until later."

Busy. Colleen sighed contentedly at the memory of what had *kept* them busy.

"We're going to make shamrock cookies for the dinner at the church," Claudie said. "You guys will have to go to town alone tomorrow."

Mike shooed his girls toward the door. "We'll talk to Maureen in the morning and see what she has in mind. Bill and Bugsy, what are you going to do now?"

"Brush our teeth," Bugsy replied.

"And go down to the kitchen for cookies," Bill challenged.

"He's lying," Claudie stated with calm conviction. "He usually does what his mom says 'cause she depends on him."

"Good man," Mike said, tossing a wave back into the room as he urged the girls out into the hallway. "See you at breakfast."

Bugsy went right into the bathroom to brush his teeth. Bill came to sit on the edge of Colleen's bed. "Will you be okay if me and Bugsy have things to do tomorrow?"

She put a hand to his knee. "Of course I will. But I'll have to be sure this is really what Maureen wants and that you'll behave for her. Six kids in a kitchen is a lot when you're trying to get things done."

"Keegan's helping, too. And, Mom," Bill said gravely, "you know I'm dependable."

"Yes, I do," she said just as gravely.

"Okay, good night." He wrapped his arms around her. "Sleep tight. I'm going to brush my teeth and I'll tuck Bugsy in."

"Thank you, Bill. You sleep well, too."

Bugsy came to kiss her good-night, then she heard Bill tucking in Bugsy the same way she did every night. He even found the ragged black stuffed dog his little brother slept with.

When Colleen heard Bill turn off the light and climb into bed, she drifted off to sleep again, feeling more relaxed than she had in years.

"IT'S TRUE," MAUREEN SAID as all her guests sat around the breakfast table while she served French toast made with sliced cinnamon rolls and sprinkled with sugar. "I'll need the kids all day, if that's all right with the two of you."

Mike and Colleen sat opposite each other at one end of the table, their children on either side of them, making faces at one another and giggling uproariously. Cassandra and her aunts occupied the middle, and a nice-looking businessman, probably in his forties, and a newly married young couple filled the other end.

Cassandra reached over Angel to touch Mike's arm. "If you're at loose ends today, my aunts are going to Springfield to deliver product and I'm free to party, too."

He smiled politely. Cassandra Miles was everything he used to think appealed to him, but suddenly didn't even nudge his interest. He'd learned from Maureen that Cassandra's aunts had formed a business that made stuffed toys and plush animals, and since she was a marketing consultant, Cassandra was helping them on their first sales trip.

She did seem to have marketing skills, Mike mused, particularly where her own attributes were concerned. Today she was dressed in clingy green wool slacks and a sweater, and her mass of dark hair hung free and fragrant.

"Thank you," he said, "but Colleen and I have plans for today."

Cassandra looked Colleen over closely. "Are you better this morning?" she asked with what sounded like concern. The underlying note in her voice suggested she was merely annoyed. "I understand you had to be carried upstairs last night after a trying evening of...sunporch sitting."

The businessman at the end of the table glanced up. Everyone else was engrossed in their own conversations.

Mike saw Colleen's eyes ignite, but she simply

stretched her arms out in front of her and said dreamily, "I'm much better, thank you. Nothing strokes the morale like being treated like a princess." Then she fixed Mike with a glance that was subtly suggestive. "Thank you," she said, her voice a decibel lower than normal.

"My pleasure," he replied in the same tone.

Cassandra put her napkin on the table and pushed her chair back. "I hope you all have a wonderful day." She smiled at her aunts, but Mike noticed tears brimming in her eyes. For an instant, he could only stare, wondering what had brought them on. She noted his attention and turned away abruptly. "I'll just make sure everything you need is in the car," she said over her shoulder to her aunts, then excused herself and walked hurriedly from the room.

Colleen looked immediately regretful.

The bride, who'd been staring daggers at Cassandra through breakfast, now leaned back guiltily in her chair.

Dolores, one of the aunts, a plump, beautifully dressed woman in her middle fifties, watched her niece retreat, then smiled apologetically around the table.

"Cassie used to be such a happy girl until her fiancé was killed in a building accident," she said.

Maureen, pouring coffee, stopped to frown. "How awful. When was that?"

"About four months ago," Dolores replied. "She's

plunged herself into helping us get our business off the ground and just hasn't taken the time to grieve.''

The smallest of the aunts, Aletha, a shy little thing with an old-fashioned air, said softly, ''She's always been so strong and so determined, I think she views her feelings of grief as a weakness and refuses to let anyone see them—even herself.''

The third aunt, taller and slender with a professorial air, nodded agreement. She was Joanne. ''She seems to engage every man she meets in conversation, as though trying to prove to herself that she's unaffected by what happened. She comes on like a seductress when she's not like that at all. At least, she wasn't before this happened.''

''I snarled at her for flirting with Sam,'' the bride said, patting her husband's arm. ''I'm sorry.''

Dolores dismissed the apology. ''Well, it's not acceptable behavior. You had a right to snarl.''

''She's an intelligent woman,'' Tom Crawford, the businessman, said. ''She knows that's the reaction she'll get. Maybe it's her way of punishing herself for being alive when the man she loved isn't.''

Everyone was silent for a moment, considering that.

Mike had seen Tom Crawford watching Cassandra. For some reason Mike didn't understand, Tom didn't seem to attract Cassandra's efforts. He was a good-looking man, tall and fit and obviously accomplished. That morning Mike had wandered out onto the back deck and found him there smoking a cigarette. He'd told Mike he was in Cooper's Corner to interview for the position of town planner.

Tom reached into the breast pocket of his suit to pull out a pack of cigarettes, which he held up to the group with a smile. "I do something similar."

"Who did you lose?" Dolores asked gently.

"My wife and teenage daughter," he replied after a moment. Something about the squaring of his shoulders suggested it had been a long road back from that dark moment. "I'd quit for my wife when our daughter was born. I started smoking again the day they died in a car accident on their way to buy a…a prom dress. That was almost three years ago." He swallowed and smiled thinly. "I'm trying to cut down."

"Good." Joanne, who was seated beside him, took the pack of cigarettes from him. "I'll help you." Then she asked pointedly, "Would you join the four of us for dinner tonight?"

"Ah…"

"Six o'clock," Dolores said. "We'll call for you." She pushed her chair back before he could refuse her, and marshaled her sisters. "Come along, girls. We don't want to be late for our appointments."

Tom grinned and stood, too. "Guess I'll be on my way since I don't have an after-breakfast cigarette to smoke."

The newlyweds remained, but they were lost in each other's eyes. Maureen took Cassandra's chair and put the coffeepot down between Mike and Colleen. "I suggest you two enjoy the luxury of a second cup of coffee and let me abscond with your children."

"They've promised us their cooperation," Colleen said with a wince, "but are you sure you want to do this? You have two three-year-olds of your own."

She nodded. "Keegan's promised to help me ride herd. We have to make fifty dozen cookies."

Colleen looked her in the eye. "And you think working with six children is going to simplify that job for you?"

"We were quite a team last night making decorations. You know, I'm not even a member of St. Bridget's congregation. I go to the Episcopalian church in town. But we're such a small community that the two parishes help each other out—and Father Gallagher's hard to resist." She leaned toward Colleen. "By the way, how're you coming with the verse?"

"I'm going out to get inspiration for it today," she said purposefully.

"Good. Well, kids. You ready?"

After goodbye kisses and hugs for Mike and Colleen, the children followed Maureen with obvious anticipation.

"I can never stir that kind of enthusiasm in Bill for cooking," Colleen said, watching them go. She reached for the pot and topped up their coffees, then leaned toward Mike. "Do you get the feeling she's trying to give us time together?"

"Yes." He nodded, sipping at the coffee. "But it's

our own fault after last night.'' He grinned. ''Or more specifically, *your* fault.''

''Hah!'' she denied with a laugh. ''If you'd let me leave when I wanted to, we wouldn't have been there to get caught.''

MIKE CONCEDED HER POINT with a very wicked smile that revved Colleen's pulse. ''You kissed me. It seemed only fair that I get to kiss you.''

''Yes, well, we'll have no more of that,'' she said with a benevolently dictatorial tone. ''Now that we've done it, we should probably just…leave it at that.''

He pushed his cup away and looked at her as though she'd advocated murder.

''What?'' he demanded quietly.

She met his gaze evenly. ''This vacation is over on Saturday. Then we go our separate ways.''

He didn't seem to see the problem. ''So? Boston is only fifty miles from New Bedford.''

She rolled her eyes. ''I'm not talking about the geographical distance. I'm talking about the…the…'' She made a rolling motion with her hand while grasping for the right words. ''The social distance.''

He shook his head as though certain he couldn't have heard her correctly. Then he asked again in that same tone, ''What?''

She sighed. She'd been thinking about this since she'd awakened at 5:00 a.m. A relationship with Mike looked so promising, but it just couldn't work. This kind of thing didn't happen to her. She was the *bad-luck* girl.

"You're a dentist," she said, "with a Back Bay address. I'm…a checker in a grocery store."

For an instant, he looked as though her sanity was in question. "What in the hell does that have to do with anything?" he finally asked.

"I'm used to being lower-middle class," she said, thinking how silly that sounded even as she spoke the words. Even sillier because they were true. "I'm happy there. I've learned that if I don't expect a lot, I don't get trampled. I'm holding my own. We're fine. I'd like to be home more for the boys, but I…I don't want to expose myself or them to…to…"

"That's such a load of tripe," he interrupted, "you can't even put the words together. What you're trying to say is that if you can't give something to the boys all by yourself, then you don't want them to have it. Isn't that it?"

It wasn't, although she knew that's what it sounded like. "No," she said. Even she thought the simple reply unconvincing.

Their heated discussion was interrupted by the appearance from the kitchen of an older man of medium height. His dark hair had a generous sprinkling of gray, and he wore stained but clean coveralls and a dark blue thermal shirt. He was almost gaunt, but sinewy, and moved with the grace of someone who was never still—even in his late fifties or early sixties.

"'Morning," the man said politely, staying at the

far end of the table. "I'm Ed Taylor, the Coopers' neighbor."

Mike stood and indicated Colleen. "This is Colleen O'Connor." He reached across the table to shake hands. "And I'm Mike Flynn."

The man sat and smiled from one to the other. "Go ahead with your fussing. Gotta get that stuff out in the open. I'll pretend I can't hear you."

Clint walked in with two steaming plates of breakfast.

"You two meet my neighbor?" he asked, placing a plate before Ed and one for himself across the table. "He provides us with the best free-range chickens this side of the Rockies."

"We've already introduced ourselves," Ed said with a smile in their direction. "They're having a spat, though. I promised we'd pretend we couldn't hear."

Clint nodded with a wide grin. "Carry on. We're too hungry to notice."

"If you'll excuse us, we'll save you from having to pretend," Colleen offered, rising from her chair.

Mike got up, too, and came around the table. "Let's get our coats," he said, "and let these men enjoy their breakfast."

She complied, but said quietly as they started away, "I'm supposed to clear my mind today for Father Gallagher's verse. If you're going to be grumpy, having you along will be counterproductive."

He ran a hand down his face. When it lingered over his mouth, she guessed it was holding back a curse.

"Would you please get your jacket," he asked with exaggerated politeness, "before I shout an obscenity within earshot of my children, or break something that doesn't belong to me?"

"My jacket is on the hook by the front door," she said, "but if you're going to pick on me, I'll leave you behind."

"You think you can outrun me?"

"I'll take my car," she said, then added as though it had just occurred to her, "Oh, that's right. My car's missing a door, because someone carelessly *pleated* it for me."

Turning her around, he pushed her gently toward the door. Once he'd helped her on with her jacket, he caught her hand and headed for the woods.

CHAPTER SIX

THOUGH IT WAS ALMOST SPRING, there was still no green visible anywhere except in the undergrowth, and the tops of the trees were just a lacy pattern of bare branches against the bright blue sky. The wind was strong and sharply cold.

Colleen stopped to zip up her jacket. Mike pulled her collar up. "The tips of your ears are already red," he said. "You should have a hood."

She started walking again. "I'll be fine. My hair's thick even though it's short."

"That doesn't help your ears."

She sent him a sidelong glance. "Neither does your continuous criticism."

He sighed. "It wasn't a criticism, it was an observation. Now, tell me again how you're teaching the boys not to expect much in life."

The glance became a glower. "That isn't what I said. I said I don't want them to learn to count on more than I can give them."

They walked side by side without touching, she forging ahead, her breath puffing out ahead of her, he slowing his pace to stay with her, hands in his pockets.

''Because we shouldn't dream, or strive to make our lives better? Because relationships *never* work? Because…''

''Because I'm what they can count on!'' she said more forcefully than she'd intended. She stopped, pointing a finger at him through the cuff into which she'd curled her cold hands. ''And don't act so self-righteous. I can't work any harder and still have time with them. I've tried going back to school, but it makes me tired and crabby and I'm still no good to them. Then I discovered that I could make a little extra with greeting card verses, and that was going really well until I just couldn't think anymore.'' She swung her arms to indicate the sunshine and their surroundings. ''And now I have this beautiful day to restore myself and you're going to spend all of it shouting at me!''

''Damn it, Colleen, somebody should shout at you. You're refusing to let a relationship develop between us because I make more money than you do?''

''Because you represent what I can't have!'' she said hotly.

''What's that?''

''Solvency! Laughter! Protection!'' Then she felt her anger deflate as she added lamely, ''Happiness.''

He caught her arm and held her in front of him. She noticed absently that the air smelled of wood smoke and some spicy natural perfume, and that his eyes were the color of a winter night. "Why?" he demanded. "Why can't you have those things?"

"I don't know," she admitted. "I just know they're not intended for me." She shrugged, unsure how to make him understand what she knew for a fact. "I'm the bad-luck girl. Everyone says so."

"That's ridiculous."

"Maybe. But it's true. If you recall, my mother died when I was eight, my father was an alcoholic and died when I was in college, my husband was charming and funny and brought this wonderful light into my life—but it turned out that he had no intention of helping *me*. He was counting on me to get *him* the things he wanted." She flung her arms out again, her hands invisible. "I'd landed a job with an ad agency in Boston, and supported us moderately well. Then there was a merger about the time Danny left. The other company was family-owned and needed jobs for all their offspring, so I was out. I got on almost right away with a small publisher, who went belly-up within months. Now my ex-husband's tending bar at some resort in Bermuda, the ad agency is still in operation, and the publisher I worked for is now doing business on the Internet, so I don't think I represent a curse to anyone else. I'm just bad luck to *myself*."

That speech delivered, she drew a breath and continued to stare into Mike's disbelieving eyes. "At heart, I know how lucky I am because I have my boys and they're healthy and relatively happy. But with my luck, I can't do anything to endanger them."

He blinked at her, shifted his weight and folded his arms. "We'll disregard the fact that you're suggesting I'm a danger to children…"

"I didn't say that!" she interrupted.

He went on as though she hadn't spoken. "…and focus on your bad luck. You have had a concentrated string of it, but that's not bad luck, it's just life. Up one minute, down the next. One step forward, two steps back. My parents are wonderful, but I lost a brother and a sister to cystic fibrosis when I was a young teenager. I did well in college, but it took me eight years because I had to alternately work a year and go to school a year. Then I met Marianne, thinking, like you did of Danny, that she was everything I wanted. She was beautiful and seemed to adore me, but for roughly the same reasons Danny wanted you. She thought I could give her the social position and material things she'd always wanted. It wasn't that I didn't like those things, but I thought it would be good to try to make a contribution to society as well. She didn't approve, finally got tired of our slow social and economic rise, and left me for a builder. You're no different from a million other people you could poll. You're just frightened by the knowledge that you can do everything right and things can still go wrong."

"Doesn't that seem as though it's contrary to…to science, or something? Like the laws of the universe should protect you from that?"

"I think the simple truth is that nothing protects

you from anything. You just do your best, keep a light on and be ready to deal with whatever happens. God does what he does and we have to cope.''

''I want my children to have more security than that.''

''You love them and care for them to the best of your ability. That's the only guarantee they get. And the world's filled with children who'd be delirious to have a fraction of the love and attention Bill and Bugsy get.''

She sighed, then took several tentative steps forward. ''I didn't say I thought you were a danger to my children.''

He started after her. ''Yes, you did. I accused you of refusing to explore a relationship and you said you didn't want to endanger your children. What else could that mean?''

When he caught up with her, she hooked her arm in his and they headed up a narrow trail flanked by fragrant pines.

''It meant,'' she said, ''that they already like you. If I spent time with you and they got to like having you around, it could all fall apart for them if we decided we weren't good together after all.''

''You mean if your bad luck kicked in.''

''We do have a lot of trouble getting along.''

''That's because you're illogical, hardheaded and hysterically self-protective.''

She pinched his arm through his coat. ''Really. I

thought it was because you were dictatorial and opinionated.''

He smiled reluctantly. ''Well, that could contrib-
ute.''

''You do realize we met less than forty-eight hours
ago.''

''That doesn't matter to me,'' he said, his voice
sounding loud as the silence of the forest enveloped
them. ''My heart knew you the minute I saw you.''

''I had tuna in my hair when you first saw me, and
I was supine on the sunporch floor.''

He grinned broadly. ''Didn't matter. Destiny
spoke.''

She sighed, wrapping both arms around him, con-
founded by the fact that for all the shouting they did
at each other, she felt closer to him than anyone. ''I'm
not sure I believe in destiny.''

''If you believe in back luck,'' he pointed out,
''you have to believe in destiny.''

''But if lovers are destined, why do we make mis-
takes like Danny and Marianne?''

MIKE STOPPED AT THE SOUND of that word. ''Lovers,'' he said, looking down into her eyes. He saw
himself reflected there. ''Is that what you want us to
be?''

A score of reactions crossed her face. She opened
her mouth to reply, then changed her mind. She finally admitted on a little sigh, ''I'm confused.''

He accepted that. It was better than *no*.

"Maybe," he said, walking on again, "we don't really understand about destiny until we meet the one we're destined for. Until then, it's just a word."

"I guess that's reasonable."

Peace established, if only temporarily, they walked hand in hand for some distance until they found an intersecting road and a sign that read To Town.

"What will inspire your creativity most?" Mike asked. "Nature?" He pointed to where the road continued through the woods. "Or civilization?"

She laughed softly. "I was just thinking that a mocha would do a lot for my frame of mind."

"Okay then." They turned onto the road to town.

The half-hour walk brought them into Cooper's Corner south of Main Street and the village green. They passed scattered homes, several advertising antiques, one an artist's residence with a small gallery in the garage. They wandered in and found a watercolor of Twin Oaks done in the summer with the flowers in full bloom, pink roses climbing a trellis on the side and clematis entwined in a pergola in the garden.

"Makes you want to come back in the summer, doesn't it?" Colleen asked, putting a finger out to touch the picture's fussy Baroque frame.

"Let's plan to do that," he said, pulling out his checkbook.

"You're not going to buy it!" she whispered with a cautious glance at the artist, who was hanging a painting on the wall behind the counter. "It must be a fortune."

He pointed to the price on the side of the frame. "It's very reasonable. And I make more than you, remember?" That last was added with humor and a trace of sarcasm.

She made a face at him. "You asked how I felt and I told you. See if I'm ever honest with you again."

He kissed her quickly. "I'm glad you were honest. Now I know you don't really hate me, that you're just a big silly."

She was ready to give him a good punch but he had the painting in his hands and she wouldn't have done anything to damage it.

They continued on their way to town, stopped at the café for the promised mocha and a scone, then went on to walk the length of Main Street. They revisited the museum they'd checked out yesterday with the children, but had time to study everything that interested them.

Colleen examined an old quilt made by a woman named Anne Burns, who'd spent an entire winter alone with her three young children after her husband failed to return from a hunting trip. She had no way of knowing that he'd been injured and was being nursed back to health by a small band of Mohicans who'd stayed behind when the tribe was moved to the Oneida Reservation in New York.

The quilt was fashioned from their old clothing,

hearts cut from Anne's husband's faded shirts and appliquéd on scraps of her dresses and the children's clothing. The quilt had been donated to the museum by one of the couple's granddaughters. She said her mother had told her that her grandmother had worked on it as a way of staying connected to her husband even though she didn't know where he was or what had happened to him. She told her children all winter long that she could still feel his love and that he'd come back to them when he could.

"Mama said that in April," the note read, "he appeared at the front door of the cabin, leaning on two Indians. The family was delirious with happiness. Grandma fed the men vegetable stew and hugged them. They acted embarrassed and finally left with muffins wrapped in a tea towel. Then she cried for an entire day."

Tears streamed down Colleen's face as she finished the Anne Burns story. "How frightening that must have been. To spend the entire winter without him, not knowing if he was dead or alive."

Mike put an arm around her and pointed out the fineness of the hand-stitching in all the small hearts made of Anne's husband's clothing.

"Her love for him was very much alive. You can see it."

She nodded. "I know, but she didn't know for *sure* that he was alive. And she still had to care for her children, chop wood for the fire and the stove, and find food. I wonder if she hunted or had enough food preserved from the summer. She must have been very brave.''

''I'm sure that's true, but it probably took more than courage to get through that winter. She must also have had faith in him and in what they meant to each other to be so sure he'd come back.''

In another case was an evening dress and a handbag that had belonged to the quilter's granddaughter. They were made of berry-red silk and covered with sequins.

''Now, she probably had a lot more fun than her grandmother did,'' Colleen speculated, feeling cheered by the festive clothing.

Mike pointed to the information printed inside the case. ''She married the governor of the state and didn't return to Cooper's Corner until she was widowed in her sixties. 'She wore this dress,''' he read from the card, '''while presiding over the annual Cooper's Corner Opera Night for Charity.' Must have been some lady. That's quite a dress for a woman her age.''

''She obviously got a lot of spirit from her grandmother.''

''Obviously.''

They explored a few more antique shops, found souvenir sweatshirts for the boys in a clothing boutique, and went back to Tubb's Café for lunch.

The restaurant was swamped with locals who probably worked nearby, day-trippers and other tourists like themselves.

A frazzled woman probably in her early sixties was clearing tables and beckoned them to a small one near the kitchen. "Hi," she said, clearly trying to be cheerful. She had kind dark eyes and short black hair too dark to be natural at her age. "Have a seat. Our waitress called in sick for the third day in a row, so we're running a little behind, but I'll bring you some coffee and get to you just as quickly as I can." She wiped off a chair sitting in the middle of the aisle and pushed it up against their table.

"You needn't hurry," Colleen assured her. "We have time."

The woman patted Colleen's shoulder. Mike noticed that her name tag read "Lori." "Bless you," she said to Colleen.

Colleen put her purchases on the floor near the wall and opened her menu. "I'm having chowder, a burger, French fries, onion rings and probably apple pie." She smiled at him over the top of the menu. "À la mode, of course. You're buying, right?"

He frowned teasingly over the top of his. "I would, but wouldn't that make me dictatorial and opinionated?"

"It'd make you gentlemanly and considerate."

"There's a double standard at work here."

She giggled. He looked up at her, unable to believe his ears. She was usually too serious to do something as carefree as giggle.

"Just kidding," she said. "I'm buying. Go all out.

Order a steak. Or the scrod. We can bring the leftovers home to my cat.''

"Why are you buying?"

She shrugged. "A rare moment of generosity. Go with it. It may never come again." She closed her menu, put it aside, then studied him across the table. "Actually, it's because I've enjoyed today so much even though you called me hysterically self-protective."

He smiled. "You are."

"I know. I guess I just appreciate that you understand that. I'm trying to loosen up, but generally I keep a tight grip on everything because I'm afraid if I don't, I'll lose it altogether."

"I do understand." He reached across the table to cover her hand. "And you're probably completely justified. It just makes it hard for me to try to get closer to you."

She opened her mouth to reply, but he thought he knew what was coming and spoke before she could. "Now, if you tell me there's no point in that because we're going our separate ways and I make more than you and am therefore a threat to your children, I *will* let you buy lunch."

"That didn't make any sense at all," she protested, tipping her head in a scolding gesture.

"That's all the sense it made when *you* said it."

Turning her hand in his, she pinched the tips of his fingers and gave him a smile that melted some resistance deep inside him. "Can't we just enjoy the rest of our visit and let the future take care of itself?"

He opened her hand to lace his fingers with hers. "Okay," he said. "But by Friday, we have to have a plan. The future doesn't take care of itself. You have to provide input—otherwise it takes off in directions you might not like."

"It does that to me all the time, anyway," she said with a shrug of acceptance.

"Okay, let's not go there again." He shook their connected hands. "We're taking charge of our lives."

She giggled again. "It sounds as though *you're* taking charge of our lives."

He put his free hand to his eyes and prayed for patience.

Their discussion was interrupted by a loud scraping noise as a slender man collided with the free chair pushed up to their table. He smiled down at them in apology. "I'm so sorry," he said. The sight of a clerical collar on the man, who had the blond good looks of a California surfer, surprised Mike. "I was just trying to get Burt's attention and didn't see the chair."

"No problem," Mike said.

Accompanying the minister was a small young woman in a woolly brown jacket that was too big for her. Her hands were joined and held close to her chest as though she'd spent much of her life trying to make herself a smaller target. She looked around warily.

"Burt!" the minister called, waving over the cashier's counter to the kitchen beyond. "Sorry to bother you when you're so busy, but here's Trudi. When I talked to Lori on the phone this morning, she said to bring her in, that your waitress hadn't shown up again."

"Can you give me two minutes, Father?" Burt's voice shouted from the back. "Just let me get this order up."

"Sure thing." The minister tried to back out of the crowded corner but was hemmed in by tables.

"Here." Mike stood and gestured the girl to his chair, then indicated that the minister take the free one. There'd been a lot of priests and ministers around his house when his siblings had been ill, and he felt great respect for them. Besides, the girl looked as though she needed a friend.

She gave Mike a hesitant smile before she sat. Her brown eyes, like her coat, looked too big for her.

The minister pulled out the chair but offered his hand before sitting down. "I'm Father Tom Christen, pastor of the Church of the Good Shepherd. This is Trudi Karr, a newcomer to Cooper's Corner."

Mike introduced himself, then Colleen. "We're tourists," he said, "staying at Twin Oaks for the week."

The man smiled. "Romantic getaway?"

Colleen giggled. Mike didn't like her reaction to the suggestion, but at least the giggle meant she was relaxed.

"We didn't know each other until we met here,"

she explained to the priest. "Mike's on vacation with his two girls, and I won a week here with my boys. They're helping Maureen make cookies for the St. Patrick's Day dinner-dance at St. Bridget's. Do you know Father Gallagher?"

"Yes, I do. We golf together when we're not competing for souls. He's Catholic. I'm an Episcopal priest."

"Father Tom?" Burt came to the counter, wiping his hands on an apron that covered a rotund body. He was balding and his head shone as though it had been scrubbed. His smile was wide and welcoming.

"Hello, Burt!"

Mike pulled out Trudi's chair and the priest caught her arm and took her with him to the counter. "This is Trudi Karr. Trudi, Mr. Tubb." Burt's big hand swallowed the girl's small one.

"Ever waited tables before?" Burt asked Trudi.

She shook her head and replied in a very small voice, "No, I haven't."

"Do you want to?"

"Yes."

Mike saw Burt measure the girl with a glance. He had to be thinking that she didn't look all that dependable. She was shy and frail, obviously not strong points for a job that required energy and personality, particularly in such a popular spot.

But a soft heart must have won out. Burt lifted a section of the counter that separated the kitchen from the front. "Well, if you don't mind starting on dishes and bussing tables, you've got the job. As you get used to things, you can start waiting tables. You'll earn tips then. Sound okay?''

The girl smiled for the first time since she'd followed Tom Christen into the café. ''Yes. Thank you.''

Tom extended his hand across the counter to Burt as Lori appeared and bustled Trudi into the back. ''Thank you, Burt. You're a good man. Giving her a job is doing God's work.''

Burt smiled wryly as he shook his hand. ''Next time you talk to God, tell him I could use a raise.''

Tom laughed. ''Sure thing. I'll be back for dinner.''

Burt turned to his grill. ''See you then, Father.''

''Thank you for your hospitality, you two,'' Tom said to Mike and Colleen. ''Hope you have a wonderful week and that I'll see you at the dance.''

They waved as he wended his way through the tables to the door.

''WHAT A NICE-LOOKING MAN,'' Colleen observed, watching him leave.

Mike put his index finger to her chin and turned it back toward him. ''You're too contentious to be a minister's wife. Will you focus on me, please? I'm the one trying to tell you that I'm a little bit in love with you.''

She smiled tauntingly. ''Just a little bit?''

''I have to know what's deep in your heart to fall

the rest of the way. And you won't let me close enough for that."

The discussion was interrupted while Lori took their order. When she was gone, Colleen folded her arms atop the table. "I have a few questions, too."

"Shoot."

"Okay. Where do you want to live when you retire?"

He was sure he'd heard her correctly, he just couldn't quite believe the question. He wondered where it fit at the moment.

"I'll answer you," he said, "but why are you worried about that when we're a good thirty years from it?"

Her question seemed to make perfect sense to her. "It tells me where your heart is. When the time comes and you can be in the absolute perfect place with just the things you want around you, where would you choose to be?"

He still wasn't sure how useful the question was, but he'd promised to answer.

"Probably somewhere tropical. I love Boston, but I'm starting to hate winter there. I like the big city, I like theater, nice restaurants, lots going on. Somewhere in Florida, maybe."

SHE KNEW IT. They had nothing in common. Florida. A big city in Florida.

He accepted her frown with equanimity and leaned

back in his chair to ask calmly, ''Not what you'd hoped for?''

''I want to live in the country,'' she told him, ''somewhere in New England. In fact, Cooper's Corner would be perfect. I love the old colonial charm, the spirit of fraternity you can feel in the air, the change of seasons, clam chowder and maple candy and blueberries.''

''Oh, now, it's not fair to use food as a wedge between us,'' he said with smiling good humor. ''These days you can get anything anywhere at any time in this country.''

''Okay, but what about the rest of it?''

''Well…if we were in love, one of us might give up what he or she wants for the other and still be very, very happy. Or by the time we're retirement age, we might both be in love with the rodeo or bird-watching, or something completely different.''

''That's silly.''

''No, it's not. You can't set limits on today because of what you think you might be headed for thirty years down the road.''

''My children will probably be in Massachusetts.''

''So might mine, but they'll have families and lives of their own, and we'll have commuter airlines and hopefully a lot of living still to do.''

''I've never been to Florida.''

''Parts of it are ugly, parts of it are beautiful. But don't you think we should date first before we decide where we're going to retire?''

She wasn't sure what she was doing. Every time she decided that Mike Flynn was quite wonderful despite everything they disagreed on, her brain seemed determined to root out all the obstacles to their relationship. She wasn't sure if she was simply trying to get them out of the way or line them up as a defense against falling in love with him.

Which she suspected she was already doing.

Their lunch arrived quickly and they talked about innocuous things while eating.

''Trudi seems afraid of her own shadow,'' Colleen said softly when they'd finished and were having a last cup of coffee. She wasn't sure if she could be heard in the kitchen or not. ''I hope she's able to keep the job.''

Mike nodded. ''I'd guess she's been abused. I've done dental work for a few women and children who were victims of abuse and they have the same characteristics—eyes darting around as though they expect a big hand to come down at any moment and knock them off their feet. Reluctant to talk. No self-esteem.''

Colleen wanted to believe Trudi would succeed. ''She's bound to do well with Tom Christen in her corner.''

''Right.'' He reached for his wallet. ''And the Tubbs seem like good people.''

''There are lots of them in this town. Put your wallet away. I said I was buying.''

He reached across the table to place a hand over

hers as she delved into her purse. She looked up at him and met a pair of very serious blue eyes. "I'm sorry. I'm physically and emotionally incapable of letting a woman pay for lunch. Or dinner."

She met his gaze with a sweet smile. "Then maybe you're going to have to change."

"That's not going to happen."

"Mike," she said patiently, "if you do want to get to know me better, and want to know what's in my heart, you're going to have to accept that I really like things my way. I know it's clear that you do, too, but that's just too bad. The gentlemanly thing to do in this instance is to let me take care of it."

Lori walked by the table and Mike handed her a couple of bills. As Colleen sputtered, he came around the table to draw back her chair. "You argue too much. I'm a man of action. The ladylike thing to do in this instance is just to accept it."

CHAPTER SEVEN

ALL RIGHT, COLLEEN TOLD herself as they walked back to the B and B, it was hard to be angry with a man determined to be kind. And particularly hard when her attraction to him was growing by leaps and bounds despite his obstinate nature.

They stopped at the corner of School and Main Streets as light traffic sped past. The wind seemed to have picked up even more, and the sky had turned to a menacing pewter color. The air was cold and sharp and vaguely reminiscent of the winter Colleen thought was behind them.

"Do you smell snow?" she asked Mike.

He caught her hand and hurried her across the street when there was a break in the traffic. "I can never smell it," he said, pointing to a clothing shop on the corner. "I always have to wait until it falls to know it's coming. I'm a city boy, remember. Let's stop in here."

"This is no time to go shopping," she argued half-heartedly. "We should be hurrying home."

He pulled her to a table near the counter where the bust of a mannequin wore a soft pink scarf and matching fuzzy earmuffs. A pair of gloves were crossed on the table in front of her. He took the earmuffs off the mannequin's head and put them on Colleen. Then he did the same with the scarf.

"Warmer?" he asked.

She couldn't deny that the earmuffs did warm her ears, which were stinging with the unexpected bite in the air.

"Yes," she said.

A clerk approached, glasses hanging from a chain around her neck. "May I help you?"

Mike handed Colleen the gloves and pulled out his wallet. "We'll take the set."

"I don't need the scarf," Colleen said. "I have…"

"And I promised to replace the sweater Chewie ruined." Mike looked around him and spotted a table of sweaters across the room. He handed the clerk his credit card, then caught Colleen's arm and drew her toward the sweaters. Beyond the large display window, snow began to drift down in large, fluffy flakes.

"Mike, it's snowing!" Colleen pointed to the window, stating the obvious.

He nodded. "Yes, I recognize it. The kids and the pets are home and safe, and you and I are on an adventure. Pick out a sweater. It was a sort of mossy green, as I recall."

She turned to tell him she'd washed it in the bathroom sink, and with a few stitches, it was going to be fine. But he was looking through a table of children's things and she'd lost his attention.

After a quick search, she found a simple turtleneck in the right color and took it to the counter. The clerk was helping him with hats and mittens for the girls and came back to the counter, a brightly colored set in each hand—one dark blue and covered in a yellow star pattern, the other light blue with white snow-flakes.

"My girls weren't prepared for this weather," he said as the clerk rang up his purchases. "Do the boys need anything?"

She shook her head. "Thanks. I usually try to be ready for everything." She went to the window to watch the snow, which was now falling in earnest. She experienced the smallest thrill at the realization that she didn't have to drive to work in it or take the boys to school. The thought of driving brought back the memory of something she'd forgotten to do.

"I should have looked for a plastic tarp to put over the back door of my car," she said, wandering back to Mike.

He glanced up from signing for his purchases. "Maybe Clint will have something you can use." He returned the pen to the clerk, picked up the large plas-tic bag and caught Colleen's hand. "You ready?"

She flung her new scarf jauntily over her shoulder. "Yes, I am." Her feet were frozen, but she was ready. She'd brought hiking boots and woolen socks, but they were back in the room. When she'd headed off on the walk this morning, she hadn't expected this. Her feet in socks and tennis shoes were cold.

Walking back to Twin Oaks hand in hand with Mike would be worth frozen feet, she thought cheerfully.

They'd just stepped out of the shop when a classic chartreuse VW Beetle pulled up in front of them. A bright yellow sign on the roof indicated it was a taxi.

Mike stared at it in alarm. "I asked the clerk to call a taxi while you were looking out the window," he said, his eyes going over the very small dimensions of the vehicle. "But I expected something...bigger."

The driver, a young blond woman in a thick parka, ran around the car to open the back door for them. "Don't look alarmed, sir. There's a trick to it. You go in sideways, one leg at a time." Her eyes ran the length of him, her words more convincing than her expression. "Where am I taking you?"

"Twin Oaks B and B," he replied.

"No problem, then. I've driven Mr. Cooper several times and he fits. I think he's got two or three inches on you."

Colleen climbed in, but Mike looked uncertain. "You didn't have to cut him up to get him in, did you?"

She laughed and held the door while he followed her instructions and climbed in after Colleen.

Once in, he turned to Colleen with a pained expression. "I think I just broke both legs. They weren't made to fold twice."

The driver laughed. "Sorry, sir. I'll try to make it quick."

Colleen wedged herself into the corner of her side to give him as much room as possible—which wasn't really much at all. He shifted to stretch out his legs and fell against Colleen as the driver turned up the hill to Twin Oaks.

She wrapped her arms around him and held him there when he would have pushed himself up. "You're fine," she said, patting his chest affectionately. "I was looking forward to the walk home, but this is even cozier."

She was surprised she'd admitted that. All her defenses seemed to be crumbling this afternoon. It must be the intimate atmosphere created by the beautiful little town and the falling snow. And the fact that there wasn't one thought or fear in her head that she hadn't shared with him today.

"Well," he said, relaxing against her, "I wish you'd told me it was coziness you were after. I'd have approached this day in a completely different way."

"No," she said, tightening her arms. "This day was perfect just as it was."

His hands came up to clasp her wrists, which were crossed over him. She felt his wiry hair against her chin, looked down on his thick, straight eyelashes, the top of his strong nose. Her gaze traveled down his flannel shirt, revealed beneath his open leather jacket, until it disappeared under the belt of his jeans. His stomach was flat, and his long legs were folded almost in half to fit in the back with her.

Awareness ran through her like chase lights on a

theater marquee. She had difficulty remembering that there was a driver in the car. She tried to recall all the arguments she'd given him all day long about why they couldn't—shouldn't—pursue a relationship. She couldn't think of one.

Getting him out of the back of the VW Bug required the efforts of both Colleen and the driver. They pulled on his arms until his upper torso and one leg were free, then supported him as he tried to retrieve the other leg still in the car.

"It's fallen asleep," he complained, holding on to the roof of the taxi. "Go on in, Colleen. Driver, you can pick up your next fare and I'll just hold on to the roof until my circulation returns. Pretend I'm not here."

The driver laughed as she and Colleen bore his weight. Snow drifted down on them, covering their heads and their shoulders, and the wind was picking up. "It must be fun to be married to someone with a sense of humor," the woman said. "My boyfriend takes himself so seriously. He'd be embarrassed by this rather than amused."

Yeah, Colleen thought. It must be. And for the first time since Danny had left, she speculated on what it would be like to be married again.

"How're you doing, sir?" the driver asked. "Can you move the leg yet?"

He groaned and dragged it out of the car, hopping backward on the free leg while the women held on to him. Colleen braced her footing on the now-slick driveway.

"Next time," he said, reaching into his wallet to pay her, "could you just strap me to the roof?"

She accepted payment and his generous tip with a pat on his arm. "You have to have antlers to ride there, sir. Thanks for calling Terri's Taxi."

She handed them their packages, then drove off with a cheerful blast of her horn.

Colleen kept her arm around Mike's waist as he limped toward the front door.

They were immediately pounced on by the children, who dragged them into the kitchen to show off the rows and rows of cookies cooling.

"We made six hundred cookies," Bill reported.

"Yeah, but we have only 588 left." Claudie held up a cookie with one of the shamrock leafs missing, suspicious tooth marks scalloping the edge. "We ate a whole bunch, to make sure they were good."

Maureen grinned. "Chewie wandered in to test them, then Tom came back from his interview, so we tried them out on him. It's unanimous. These are Cordon Bleu-quality cookies."

Colleen pulled off her gloves. "Shouldn't Mike and I try them to make it unanimous?"

Bugsy held up one in each hand. He was dusted in flour. "Tomorrow we're gonna frost 'em!"

Colleen couldn't help but wonder what he'd look like under a coating of green icing.

Angel suddenly burst into the kitchen, wearing her

coat and boots. "Hi, Daddy! Can we go outside and make a snowman? Maureen didn't want to let us go until you came home to say it was okay."

"Sure." He took one of the bags he'd dropped on a kitchen chair and pulled out their hats and gloves. "But you'd better wear these. And you have to stay in the backyard where we can see you."

"Mom, can we go, too?" Bill pleaded.

"Yes. Same rules apply, though. You have to stay in the back."

"Right!" He started off, then noting the other bag on the chair, asked, "Did you bring *us* something?"

She shook her head. "No. I forgot about you entirely."

Bugsy wrapped his arms around her. "You never do that."

She feigned reluctance. "Oh, all right. I brought you each a Minuteman sweatshirt."

"Cool!" they said in unison as they grabbed the bag and ran for the stairs.

The girls had a momentary squabble over who got which hat and mittens.

"I want the dark blue one!" Claudie pouted as Angel tried to claim it.

Mike rolled his eyes.

Munching on her cookie, Colleen said casually, "I think the light blue one's more mature."

Claudie kept her grip on the dark blue one, considered for a moment, then snatched the light blue set and ran upstairs.

"That was pretty slick," Mike praised quietly as Maureen used kitchen shears to cut the tags off Angel's hat and mittens. "Thank you."

Colleen shrugged off the compliment. "She's a woman, and age is a woman thing. It's just that at her age, you want to be considered older. The whole thing changes direction at about thirty-five. Excuse me. I'd better go check on *my* Chuie."

"I have meat loaf in the oven," Maureen said, catching Colleen's attention before she left the room. "Just in case the weather gets too bad for our guests to go into town for dinner."

"That's thoughtful, thank you. The boys love meat loaf."

Mike nodded, helping Angel on with her hat. "So do the girls and I."

"Mashed potatoes and gravy and green beans?" Maureen asked.

"Yum!" Angel approved.

The boys were already running down the stairs, coats flying, when Colleen started up. She opened her mouth to caution them to settle down, but knew it would be futile. After all day in the kitchen—apparently working hard—they were due to blow off a little steam.

When she reached the top of the stairs, one of the doors at the other end of the hall opened and Cassandra stood in the doorway in pink sweats, her hair disheveled, her eyes red.

"Oh. Sorry," she said. "I heard a lot of footsteps. I thought you might be my aunts."

Remembering what Cassandra's aunts had said about her this morning, Colleen felt compelled to reach out to her. "That was my boys. They always sound like an invading army. You didn't go with your aunts?"

Cassandra assumed the look of hauteur that had kept Colleen at bay since she'd arrived, then it seemed to collapse on itself and she shook her head. "No. They know what they're doing, and I just wasn't up to their..." She stopped, seemingly reluctant to say anything negative, then finished with a sigh, "Their pervasive good cheer."

Colleen smiled and took a step toward Cassandra's door. "I know what you mean. I hate attempts to cheer me up when I'm not in the mood."

Cassandra almost smiled, but not quite. "Snow's really coming down."

"Yes. The kids were going out to build a snowman."

"I'm not sure my aunts know how to drive in this." Cassandra leaned a shoulder in the doorway. "They've been living in Florida for the past fifteen years or so."

"Where did they go?"

"They had appointments in Williamstown and Bennington, Vermont, right over the border. It's only about thirty miles away, but they're very gentle ladies."

"I know." Colleen realized Cassandra was very worried about them. "Are they carrying a cell phone?"

She nodded. "It doesn't answer." Then she straightened and took a step back into the room. "Well. I'm sure you have things to do."

Colleen took another step toward her, wanting to help. "Do you want to go down to the kitchen for a cup of coffee? Maybe we could call the state police, ask them to keep an eye out for their car."

The other woman shook her head. "No thanks on the coffee. And I can't really say they're overdue. If business was going well, it could just be taking time. I'm hoping I'll hear from them soon. Or they'll just walk in the door."

"Yes. I'll hope for that, too. If there's anything I can do..."

Cassandra stared at her a moment as though Colleen puzzled her. "You and Mike Flynn have a good time?"

"We did. We just looked through shops and the museum and had lunch..."

Cassandra started to pull the door closed, clearly determined to keep Colleen at bay. She nodded. "He's the type that makes you feel...safe."

That was true. Colleen was aware of that every moment, in spite of their antagonism.

Her eyes unfocused, Cassandra said, "I remember how that felt."

Colleen wanted to tell her she was sorry about her

fiancé, but Cassandra excused herself and shut the door completely.

Fu Manchu had not even noticed Colleen was gone. She was curled up on the pillows, one paw stretched out. When Colleen walked over to her, she rolled over obligingly for a stomach rub, then remained in that position and drifted off to sleep again.

Colleen went to the window to look out at the falling snow. It drifted in silence, the sight calming and beautiful. She told herself Cassandra's aunts could not be in any trouble. It was too beautiful to be dangerous.

And for once, she could enjoy watching the snow fall without worrying about going anywhere. She could just watch it fall and feel...

Her gaze drifted to the end of the parking area visible from her window and she was surprised by the empty spot. Where was her car? She leaned closer to the window, which was cold as an ice cube, and tried to see around the house. Mike's van was there, but where was *her* now air-conditioned little car?

She went downstairs and out the front door, pausing just long enough to count cars. Empty space where the aunts' rental should be, empty space where the honeymooners' little compact had been before they'd left, Tom Crawford's red four-by-four, Mike's van, empty space. She looked across the lot and saw Maureen and Clint's vehicles.

"Where's my car?" she asked the falling snow.

She ran back into the house, headed for the kitchen

and noticed Mike lying on his back on the carpet in front of the fire. A sudden suspicion began to form.

Hands on her hips, she stood over him. "Where's my car?"

"Cooper's Corner Automotive Service," he replied without opening his eyes. "It'll be back by Friday."

She knelt beside him and swatted his arm. "I told you I would..." she began hotly.

He caught her by the shoulders, pulled her down onto the carpet beside him and pinned her there, one arm across her chest.

"And I couldn't just let you drive home without a door." He propped a forearm on the carpet and leaned over her, his expression firm. "Please don't give me a lot of grief about it. You can pay me back."

"It'll take me twenty years!"

"I've got time."

She was angry.

And maybe she wasn't, really.

It was hard to analyze precisely what she felt. She didn't want to be indebted to anyone, which was why she'd specifically refused his offer to help with the car. It was annoying to be countermanded. But she was sure his intention had simply been to help, to extend a kindness, and in that respect, it was difficult to think of the gesture as anything but generous.

Still, she was aware of the safe harbor he provided. She found herself wanting to give in and shelter there.

"I know, I know," he said with good-humored exasperation. "You don't want to trust me because your father and your ex failed you, and I'm bad luck and a danger to your children.''

She shook her index finger at him. ''If you say that one more time…'' she threatened.

He grinned. ''Yeah? What are you going to do?''

She raised her head off the floor until they were nose to nose. ''I'll put you in the back of Terri's Taxi and pay her to drive you around until your legs never straighten out again.''

He pretended a frown. ''Now, that's just mean.''

The lights overhead flickered, and the sound of the furnace, a quiet, humming undertone, ceased for one long moment. Then it continued again.

''Uh-oh,'' Colleen said. ''Are we losing power?''

''Us?'' Mike asked. ''Or the house?''

She gave his ribs a pinch. ''Would you get off me so I can check on the children?''

''You didn't answer me.''

''The power between us never flickers,'' she finally admitted. ''And that's the problem.''

HER ADMISSION SO STUNNED him that he lost focus for a moment and she was able to scramble out from under him.

He sat up, stared into the fire, and had to admit to himself that he wasn't doing very well. She was interested in him and had admitted there was ''power'' between them. He'd even go a step further and say that he thought she cared about him. That moment in the back of the cab when she'd wrapped her arms around him had been filled with tenderness as well as sizzle.

On the other hand, they'd met only three days ago. He could understand her reluctance to pursue a relationship if she felt as though she didn't know him. But that wasn't it. She was comfortable with him and had no difficulty telling him what was on her mind.

He'd understand if she didn't like his children or he didn't like hers. But his girls adored her and she seemed to like them, and he thought her boys were great.

It had to be about trust. She'd been used and abandoned by both the men in her life, and had become a force unto herself—needing no one, counting on no one. Now that she'd perfected the role of emotional and material provider, it was out of the question that she would unbend sufficiently to rely upon someone else.

And while that realization took a swipe at his ego, since he considered himself very trustworthy, it was the issue he had to defeat if he was going to be able to spend time with her once this week was over.

It occurred to him that he had to approach this from a different angle. He had to offer a relationship that didn't require she trust him.

He studied the flames, wondering if that was possible. Even the most casual of friendships required belief that the other person would be there when needed.

Maybe, he thought, running his thumbnail along his

bottom lip, that was where he was making his mistake. True love was merely real friendship carried to a physical level. It required complete trust.

But an open-ended relationship that required no commitment and was only about having fun together and making love required nothing. It was about taking rather than giving.

He couldn't decide whether to loathe himself for coming up with the idea or to congratulate himself for conceiving of a relationship she might be willing to support.

He'd have to approach it carefully. He hoped he was a good-enough actor. Then he remembered that he often told Mrs. Holland that her twins were adorable little angels. He could do this.

THE CHILDREN CAME IN drenched and had to be warmed in hot bathtubs and changed into fresh clothing. Everyone but the aunts, who still hadn't been heard from, gathered around the table for meat loaf and all the fixings.

Cassandra was visibly worried and only played with her food.

"I'll call the state police right now," Maureen said, pushing away from the table. "They haven't been missing that long, but we can ask the police to keep an eye out for their car."

"I'll call." Clint was already up and on his way to the kitchen.

"I'll drive the road to Williamstown," Mike said. "See if there's any sign of them."

Tom Crawford pushed his plate away. "I'll do it. I've got the four-wheel drive. And no pretty little girls to worry about me."

"You can't bring three older women back in the bed of your truck," Maureen argued.

"Sure I can. I've got a canopy, and there's a sleeping bag and a couple of blankets. Besides, there's only one main road to Williamstown. If they're on it, I'll find them."

"I'm coming with you," Cassandra declared as he pushed his chair back and stood.

"I don't think so," he replied.

She got to her feet and dropped her napkin on the table. "It isn't your choice."

"Pardon me," he said, facing her, "but it's my truck."

She leaned toward him across the table. "And they're my aunts. You probably don't even remember the car, or what they look like, or what they were wearing when they left."

He folded his arms. "It was a burgundy Mercedes. I do recall what they look like because they all look like each other, except that one's very small, one's buxom, and the other's tall and slender. And I don't recall what they were wearing, but the tall one is always in lavender."

Cassandra stood silent, surprised.

"My daughter loved lavender," he explained with

an uncomfortable shifting of his weight. "I always notice it. I also noticed you wear those amethyst earrings all the time."

As if in response, Cassandra raised both hands and touched the little gold flower-shaped earrings with amethyst centers.

"They were a gift from a friend," she said with a swallow.

"Your fiancé?" he asked.

Again, she looked surprised. "Yes."

The lights went off for an instant, then flicked on again.

"I'm getting my coat," Cassandra said, and hurried upstairs.

"I'll get you a jug of coffee and something to nibble on," Maureen offered, then disappeared into the kitchen.

When Cassandra came down, she was wearing a black blazer.

Tom looked dubious. "That's very fashionable, but not very warm."

"Well, I usually dress for business meetings," she snapped at him, "not for hiking across the tundra."

"I'll get you something, Cassandra," Colleen said, going to the hooks by the front door.

"There's no tundra in Massachusetts," Keegan corrected.

"What *is* tundra?" Claudie asked.

"It's land with no trees on it," Keegan explained.

"They have it in Russia and Canada, I think. It's always frozen underneath."

"You don't have a heater in your truck?" Cassandra asked Tom.

"I do," he replied patiently, "but if we get stuck, running the motor to produce heat will cause carbon-monoxide poisoning."

"Are you expecting to get stuck?"

"I like to plan for a worst-case scenario."

Colleen was back with her coat and the hat, scarf and mittens Mike had bought her that afternoon. She helped Cassandra into the coat. "It's still a little damp from our walk, but the lining's dry. And these are nice and warm." She draped the scarf around Cassandra's neck and handed her the hat and gloves.

Cassandra seemed taken aback by Colleen's generosity. Colleen gave her a quick hug. "Good luck. Call us once in a while so that we know you're all right."

Mike and Clint donned jackets and walked Tom and Cassandra out to the truck to scrape the windshield and shovel the drive behind them while Tom warmed up the motor.

The women and children gathered in the doorway to wave them off.

"I hope those ladies are okay," Claudie said worriedly. "They were really nice."

"They might have gone somewhere to have a cup of coffee until the snow stopped," Maureen suggested, frowning as the car disappeared into the storm.

"But you're supposed to call if you're going to be late," Claudia protested.

"I know."

"They probably had an accident," Bill predicted.

Colleen silenced him with a stern look. "We're thinking positive, Bill."

"Come on, let's finish dinner." Maureen ushered everyone back to the table.

"We're going to believe that they're fine," Colleen said, getting the boys settled again and resuming her chair, "and that they're just out of touch because of the snow. Now, eat up. Then we'll have a nice quiet evening watching television or reading."

The moment she'd finished speaking, the lights went out. There was silence as everyone waited for them to come on again, but nothing happened.

Maureen went to the front window and swept the curtain back. There wasn't a light to be seen anywhere in the town below, and the furnace was silent.

"I hope somebody has books in braille," Bill said dryly.

CHAPTER EIGHT

MAUREEN TOUCHED A MATCH to the candles on the table, then to the tapers in the wall sconces on either side of the fireplace.

Mike and Keegan went outside to bring in more wood while Clint stoked the fire from a cheerful little dance into a serious heat-making flamenco.

Tom phoned the inn at eight to report that they were in Williamstown and hadn't seen a sign of the aunts' car. They were about to check in at the police station and would call back if there was any news. Otherwise, they'd call in another hour.

Maureen, who'd picked up the phone, gave the others the report in a tone that said "no news is good news."

Clint carried wood upstairs to build a fire in the Flynns' room. "You and the boys may as well stay down here," Maureen suggested to Colleen. "We'll bring down your blankets and pillows—there are enough chairs and couches and the twins and I can spread out on the floor."

Mike shook his head. "The twins can have my bed. I'll stay down here."

Maureen was adamant. "Now, what kind of an inn-keeper would I be if I let a guest sleep on the floor?"

"A cooperative one," he replied.

Clint made a scornful sound when he came back downstairs. "Well, you misjudged her there, Mike. Smart, savvy, sometimes sweet, but never coopera-tive. At least not without a lot of argument."

"Hmm," Mike answered with a smiling side glance at Colleen. "Something women have in com-mon."

"Only because they all have to deal with men," Colleen put in as she helped Maureen clear the table.

"I can do this," Maureen said, trying to take the stack of dishes from her. "You're not supposed to work."

"And you're not supposed to cook dinner," Col-leen argued, holding a firm grip on the dishes, "but you did so that we wouldn't have to go out in this weather. The least I can do is help you with the dishes." And she marched past her hostess into the kitchen.

Maureen turned to the men and pointed after Col-leen with a grin. "Well, you might be right about *her*."

Once the dishes were done, Colleen and her boys, Mike and his girls, and Clint, Maureen and Keegan sat in a large circle on the living room floor playing word games. The twins had fallen asleep in a big chair near the fire, and Claudie, like a little mother, had covered them with a blanket. Chewie was sacked out in front of the fire, his big body radiating heat, and Fu Manchu lay in a tight little ball on the back of the chair the twins occupied.

Tom called again at nine with nothing new to report.

Bugsy had curled up with his head on Colleen's knee and fallen asleep. Angel fought sleep, thrilled at being allowed to participate in the challenging game. She blinked, her eyelids closed heavily, then she blinked again and finally leaned against Mike with a wide yawn.

"I'd better take these guys upstairs," Mike said as he noticed Claudie's efforts to stay awake. "Maureen, I'd feel so much better if you'd…"

She was already shaking her head. "I have a million things to do to prepare for the morning. And this happened to us a couple of times this winter. The living room's perfectly comfortable for sleeping. The twins don't look at all deprived, do they?"

Everyone turned to the big overstuffed chair where both girls were curled up side by side, fast sleep.

"No, I have to admit they don't," he said, then turned to Colleen. "I insist that you and the boys take my bed."

"Thanks, but we…" she began to demur. Bill was already racing up the stairs. "His bed has drawers underneath! It's really cool!"

Bugsy sat up sleepily. "What's going on?" he asked.

"We get to sleep in Mike's bed tonight!" Bill shouted down at him.

"Wow!"

Suddenly awake, Bugsy followed him up at a run.

Colleen turned to Mike, her mouth open to speak, the situation completely out of her hands.

He nodded slowly. "I just learned something from them. If I want you to see things my way, the trick is not to give you a chance to speak. Come on. Would you help Claudie?"

The dog stirred to follow, and Claudie drowsily reached for the cat. "We made friends. She likes it if I scratch her under the chin," she told Colleen.

HOW COULD SHE REFUSE to help a sleepy child up the stairs to bed? Colleen wanted no part of letting her children sleep in Mike's bed, because she was going to end up in the room, too. She just knew it. The problem was, she really wanted to—so she didn't dare.

Mike put Angel in one of two cots placed side by side near the fire, then Colleen took Chuie from Claudie as he helped her climb into the cot beside her sister's.

When he'd finished tucking them in, Chuie scrambled out of Colleen's arms and leapt onto Claudie's stomach. Claudie yawned, then smiled. "I told you she likes me." Then she closed her eyes.

Colleen went to her boys, who'd climbed into Mike's bed. Bugsy knelt on a pillow, studying the elaborate carving on the headboard, while Bill lay on his side close to the bedside table, where a laptop computer rested.

"Don't touch!" Colleen warned in an urgent whisper.

Bill looked offended. "I wasn't going to. I just think it's cool that he has one. What's in there?" he asked Mike, who came to the bedside.

"Notes about some of my patients," Mike explained. "My accounts receivable…"

"What's that?"

"Patients who owe me for the work I've done for them."

"Oh."

"My calendar to help me remember where I'm supposed to be and when. Birthdays and phone numbers I want to remember."

"Can you check your e-mail?"

"Yes."

"We don't have e-mail 'cause we don't have a computer. They're too expensive. I might get one for my birthday, but that's not till September."

"Do you use them at school?"

"Yeah. I really like it, too. I know how to write stuff and use the spell checker. And I know how to play some of the games."

"Well, by the time you get one, you should be really good at it. But you have to remember to go outside once in a while and shoot hoops."

Bill grinned and rolled onto his back. "I'd never forget that. Thanks for letting us use your bed."

"Sure."

Bugsy slid down with a bounce and got under the covers. "Yeah. Our beds at home are bunk beds," he grumbled, "and Bill gets to sleep on top 'cause Mom's afraid I'll fall out."

Mike tucked the boys in with the ease of experience, then walked around to Bugsy's side of the bed. "I'm sure she wouldn't want that to happen. And it could if you had a wild dream about flying, or something."

Bugsy sat up abruptly. "I need Blackie."

"Who?"

"His stuffed dog," Colleen explained, pushing the door open that connected their rooms and going into hers. She found the dog in the middle of Bugsy's cot and hurried back to him with it. He held it tightly in his arm and his eyelids swept down slowly.

"Thanks, Mom. G'night," he said on a deep sigh.

"Good night, sweetheart." She kissed his cheek and walked around the bed to kiss Bill's forehead. "You be very quiet, okay," she said softly. "The girls are already asleep."

"Okay," Bill whispered.

Colleen straightened and braced herself to face Mike. Every nerve she possessed pulsed in awareness of him. She knew she couldn't sleep now if she was sedated, then hit over the head with a skillet.

"I'd like to talk to you about something," he said quietly. "Can we go into your room?"

She wanted to appear relaxed, controlled. "Of course. I'll make a pot of coffee." Then she remembered. "Oops," she said. "No power."

He smiled. "I know. I keep hitting light switches. Do you have candle sconces in your room, too?"

"Yes. One near the door to the hallway, and another above the dresser." She pushed the door open wide so that the neighboring firelight provided some light. Mike walked in and lit both sconces with the utility lighter from his room.

There was a definite chill in the air, though keeping the door open between the rooms helped a little.

Colleen took a blue hooded sweatshirt out of her closet and tried to shrug into it. Mike came to help her when the fleece lining dragged against her sweater and refused to slip on.

He was very close, touching her arms, her shoulders. Reaching inside the sweatshirt at her wrist, he pulled down on her sweater as he pulled up on the shoulder of the sweatshirt. His knuckles were warm against her quickening pulse.

"You should get something warmer to put on," she said with excessive brightness, sure her portrayal of a woman in control was fooling no one. "It's freezing in here. It's too bad about the coffee. I'd have loved a cup. I can drink caffeine all day long and it doesn't keep me awake. I always have a cup before bed. Hazelnut praline."

He winced. "Girl stuff."

She puttered with the zipper on her sweatshirt. "Girl stuff? What's with you and my boys, anyway? I thought we were working toward a genderless society—at least as far as defining the things we can do and be. But my boys insist that we always have girl fun instead of guy fun."

He nodded as though he understood. "Shopping, museums, walks, movies rather than sports that are played to the death."

She wanted to laugh, but she was too tense, too charged to unbend. So she kept talking. "I'm trying to raise a pair of civilized boys and it's not going to help if they hear you endorsing the 'girl-fun'-'guy-fun' theory. I just don't want boys who chew and spit and swear. I don't see why men can't be masculine without doing all kinds of disgusting things. I mean, it's possible to…"

"Colleen…" He stood and picked up a brightly colored quilt off the foot of the bed and held it open. "Come here," he invited.

She considered that open blanket, knew it represented both warmth and danger, and wondered whether or not to take the risk. But she was out of breath, anyway, so she went to him.

Standing behind her, he wrapped her in the quilt and held it closed by encircling her with his arms. When he lowered his head, his cheek touched hers for a moment, and she leaned backward into the embrace, unable to stop herself.

The moment seemed to stretch out endlessly, then he sat her down on the edge of the bed.

"I want you to relax," he said gently, leaving a small space between them before sitting down.

She wrapped her hands in the blanket to hold it to her, touched by the thoughtful gesture. "You mean you *aren't* trying to seduce me?" she teased.

He grinned, but there was something serious in his eyes. "Of course I am, but I'm trying to take the fear out of it for you."

She had to respect his honesty. But it certainly destroyed any illusions she had about thinking she could behave like a woman in control.

"How do you plan to do that?" she asked in a breathless voice.

"By making an old-fashioned proposition."

Ask a silly question... "Proposition?"

"Yes." He turned slightly to face her, one leg bent and resting on the bed, the other braced on the floor. "There's something electric between us. Nuclear, even. Are we agreed on that?"

That required no thought. "Yes."

"But you've had bad experiences with men and aren't willing to take a chance on another one."

She could split hairs on that, but essentially, her answer was "Yes."

"So, if I understand your concerns correctly, you like being with me, but you don't want to pursue a relationship because you don't want to end up making a commitment you're sure you'll ultimately regret."

That sounded judgmental and cold-blooded, but again her answer was "Yes."

"Then let's take all the danger out of it for you."

She was afraid to ask, but had to. "How?"

"By removing the threat of commitment."

The *threat* of commitment. She felt small, realizing that she did consider promising to be there for someone a threatening situation. She didn't think she knew how, when no man had ever been there for her.

"How do we do that?"

"Make it a simple, no-strings affair." He said it easily, the last word hanging in the air between them.

She repeated it, fascinated. "Affair." It sounded sophisticated yet wicked.

"Affair," he said again. "No suggestion of permanence, because you don't trust me, and I understand that."

She opened her mouth to correct him, but he was still talking. "No living together, because that still requires a level of trust and would involve the children, which isn't a good idea, since mine adore you and I think yours are great. We don't want them to be with us when we're together so they don't get the idea that it'll be permanent."

That sounded both logical and ominous.

"So what you're suggesting is just…"

"Sex," he replied with obvious satisfaction. "Well, it'd probably never be *just* physical with us because we have too much fun together. I guess you could consider it sex with affection. Liking rather than loving. No suggestion of commitment or permanence, just fun for the moment. Until I disappoint you or we tire of each other.''

She now wished someone *would* come along with a skillet.

The notion was either insane or brilliantly inspired.

''Only problem I can see,'' he went on, ''is that since it would be solely about sex, we should probably have it first to see if we're compatible. Otherwise there'd be no point, would there? We can just go our separate ways on the weekend.''

Her brain was spinning and she fought to call her thoughts into order. On the one hand, she had to admire his determination. He'd countered her objections and still found a way to pursue a relationship.

On the other hand, she couldn't help but feel his proposal was insulting. Though what else could he offer within the parameters she'd set?

She saw the future unroll before her in her mind's eye. The boys growing up, going off to school, getting married, moving away. Could she live that long without intimacy, or would she have to put pride aside and realize there was no insult in his offering sex if that was all she would allow?

But…if she was thinking about Mike Flynn being beside her as her boys grew and her life unfolded, that implied a certain permanence, didn't it? And permanence required commitment.

She understood her feelings of hurt and disappointment over the offer. She was in love with Mike Flynn.

She didn't want to be, knew it wasn't wise to be, and would give anything *not* to be, but there it was.

Still, that didn't mean she had to trust him enough to let him know.

She had an overwhelming desire to scream.

MIKE COULD TELL BY the tumult in those magic-making eyes that he was getting somewhere. This was going to work, if she didn't kill him for suggesting it.

He had no doubt that if they made love once, she would see that her fate was sealed. He was hers and she was his, permanence, commitment, joint income tax, the whole enchilada.

It was sneaky, but he was desperate.

He almost withdrew the suggestion when he caught a quick glimpse of hurt in her eyes, then she seemed to rethink the offer, and the hurt was replaced by frowning consideration.

"Take your time to think about it," he said. "We have a few more days."

She studied him with a look that went straight through him. For one awful moment, he wondered if she saw his trickery.

"And you wouldn't hate me for holding us to that?" she asked. "I mean, when you seem so eager to…to have a family life again?"

"Of course not," he replied with credible good humor. "I think we have a lot to offer each other, and if we have to do it without promise or purpose, so be it.''

She closed her eyes and wrapped herself more tightly in the blanket.

''So, I'd never see your girls, and you'd never see my boys?'' she asked.

He nodded. ''Well, that seems best, don't you think? They'd never be able to understand this kind of arrangement. Kids think in terms of outcomes. They'd be looking for something to happen.''

''Like a wedding.''

''Most likely. My girls have been on the lookout for someone for me for a while. Best not to stir that pot.''

Her shoulders were sagging and she was staring at nothing. He wanted to think that was good.

''We'd have to have sex before Friday,'' she said, still staring. ''That's the night of the dance, then I'll have to pack…''

She could be a cold-blooded little beggar. ''Yes, I suppose.''

''Do you have protection?'' She met his eyes directly.

He felt the shock of their connection. She was serious. His heart worked a little harder. ''Yes, I do.''

She smiled thinly. ''I don't take anything. Haven't needed it since Danny left.''

''That's been a long time,'' he observed sympathetically.

She shrugged. ''It didn't really seem so long. I

mean, it was nice when I had sex—at least in the beginning.'' Her eyes lost focus again and she smiled wistfully. Then the smile dissolved and she tightened her grip on the blanket as she glanced his way. ''The parts I miss, I missed even when Danny and I were still together. The tenderness, the eagerness to give, the wonderful comfort of knowing you're loved. So what he took with him when he left was already gone, anyway.''

He was tempted to hit her over the head with the revelation she'd just made. He wondered if she realized she'd just described lovemaking rather than sex, and that the wonderful comfort of knowing you were loved came only with commitment and permanence.

She stood up, probably preparing to leave, when they heard a wild commotion downstairs.

Wasting no time, she went to her door and opened it. There was only darkness beyond, but Dolores's voice drifted up to them, high and excited.

''By the time we dragged Joanne out of the bookstore, it was snowing like the sled scene in *Dr. Zhivago!* So we were almost home and just creeping along when a small pickup lost it on a turn and slid into us. Fortunately, he was going slowly, too, and just shoved us off the road.''

Mike and Colleen went carefully down the dark stairs to the gathering room to find Cassandra's aunts wrapped in blankets and Clint adding more wood to the fire. The scene looked like something from another time—candles scattered around the room for light and blankets for warmth.

"Fortunately, no one was hurt. Aletha tried to call the police on our cell phone, but the battery had died." She cast a scolding glance at the offending sister. "We're going to have to keep better track of that if we're going to be traveling around like this."

Aletha nodded. "I know. I'm sorry. I'm technologically challenged. I just learned to retrieve our messages and thought I'd accomplished something wonderful. I keep forgetting the thing works on a battery."

Dolores sipped at a cup of coffee. "Anyway, a kindly state trooper drove us home. We were afraid Cassandra would be frantic." She looked around. "Don't tell me she just went to bed."

"She and Tom went looking for the three of you," Clint said, dusting his hands off on his jeans as he came toward them. "You didn't see them?"

The atmosphere changed from cheerful relief to fresh concern.

"Oh, no," Joanne said. "It's awful driving out there."

Then the telephone rang. Clint picked up a cordless receiver from the nearby coffee table. He listened a moment, then smiled at the group. "Tom, thank God! The aunts are home, but we're all worried about you. Where are you?"

Everyone breathed a sigh of relief.

Clint held his hand over the mouthpiece. "They ran

out of gas. A state trooper drove them to Williamstown, to stay the night, then another car skidded into
theirs in the parking lot of the motel. It's going to be
towed in the morning.'' He listened again. ''He
doesn't want anyone to try to come and get them
because streetlights are out and it's too dark to see
your way.''

The aunts exchanged looks of mingled relief, surprise and speculation.

''Is Cassie all right?'' Dolores asked.

Clint relayed the question to Tom.

The answer was brief and made Clint smile. ''She's
fine,'' he told the aunts. Mike suspected the reply had
been a little more involved than that.

''I'll pick them up in the morning,'' Mike offered.

''All right,'' Clint said to Tom. ''Stay safe. Mike
says he'll come and get you in the morning. Okay.
I'll tell him. Good night.'' Clint hung up the phone
and heaved a sigh. ''Tom said to thank you, Mike.
They're both fine. Tom says the motel is comfortable.
I love happy endings.'' He smiled. ''Can I get anybody anything?''

Mike pointed to the aunts' steaming cups. ''How'd
you make coffee?''

''Oh.'' Clint pointed to the pot dangling from a
hook over the fire. ''You want some? It's instant, if
that's all right.''

''I'd love a cup. Colleen?''

''Oh, me, too!'' she exclaimed.

They all sat around the fire wrapped in blankets

and drinking coffee as the aunts retold their story from different points of view.

"I hope Cassandra's not being too difficult," Aletha said worriedly. "Mr. Crawford seemed to have her number."

Mike remembered their verbal exchange before the two set off together tonight and turned to Colleen, who waggled an eyebrow.

"But he's the only man she hadn't paid any attention to," Maureen observed.

Clint leaned back in his chair. "That's probably significant. She worked on Mike and me because she knew we weren't available."

Maureen frowned at him. "How so? You're both single."

"Because I made it clear I wasn't interested when I was changing the upstairs light bulb, and Mike is with Colleen."

Mike waited for Colleen's indignant objection, but it never came.

Maureen angled Mike a surprised glance, then turned back to her brother. "So, she was really attracted to Tom but didn't do anything about it for fear he was available?"

Clint shrugged. "As much as anyone can understand a woman's mind, I'd say maybe. She was attracted to him but didn't want to be because she thinks she isn't ready. Something like that."

Maureen patted her brother's shoulder. "You have

unplumbed depths, Clint. You're wasted as a single guy.''

"Yeah, right.'' He pushed himself to his feet. "I'd better put more water in that pot. We may all be eating instant oatmeal for breakfast. Sorry I can't offer seconds on the coffee, but that was it.''

Colleen held up her empty cup. "It was ambrosia. Thank you, Clint.''

"Sure.''

Everyone stood and said their good-nights. The aunts went up to their room and Mike followed Colleen to his, where they checked on the children. They were all fast asleep, curled up tightly in their blankets, the cat now on Claudie's pillow.

Chewie still lay in front of the fire and moved only minimally when Mike added another log and stirred the embers until it took. The dog sprawled out again and Mike patted his formidable chest. His tail thumped happily.

Mike pointed Colleen to the small slipper chair and footstool on one side of the fireplace. "If you can make yourself comfortable there, I'll get you a blanket from your bed.''

Without giving her a chance to argue, he went past her into her room, snatched the coverlet off the bed and was heading back with it when he found her obstructing his path.

She pushed the door closed and, her voice husky in the flickering shadows, said, "I have another idea.''

CHAPTER NINE

HIS HEART STALLED. He stopped where he stood. "I'm all ears," he said.

She came toward him, mummified in the quilt, her cap of red-blond hair picking up the flickers of candlelight. "Maybe we should do this tonight," she whispered, and he couldn't determine if she was afraid of waking the children, or if she simply didn't want to hear the words aloud.

He wanted to hear them. "This?" he asked.

"Sex," she said, tilting her chin up, "with affection."

Again, he couldn't determine if she was chiding him for that description of their proposed relationship, or trying to give herself its fullest value in the hope that would be enough.

He put the coverlet back on the bed, sure that whatever they called their relationship, it would be more than she could imagine. It existed already in his imagination and in his heart.

Leaning down at the head of the bed, he drew back the blankets. When he turned back to her, he saw that she remained at the foot of the bed, still clutching tightly to the quilt. The room was no longer simply chilly, but downright cold.

"You're not sure?" he asked, maintaining an outward appearance of calm while his body panicked, afraid she was thinking better of the whole notion.

She took several steps toward him. "I'm only sure that I have to know what making love with you would be like."

"You mean having sex."

"With affection. Yes."

He closed the distance between them, smiling. "Well, I don't think we can do it with you wearing the quilt."

She returned his smile tentatively. "You're sure? I really hate to part with it."

The kiss he pressed to her lips was gently teasing. She tasted of coffee and filled his nostrils with the scent of flowers. "We may be able to deal with the quilt," he joked, fascinated by her mouth and kissing it again. "But the sweats you're wearing underneath are definitely going to be a problem."

"If you hold the quilt," she bargained, kissing him back, "I'll dispense with the sweats."

"Deal." He held the two ends of the quilt together while she toed off her slippers and socks, then shrugged out of the sweatpants. Her head disappeared for an instant as she maneuvered inside the blanket, then she reappeared, her cheeks flushed, her hair mussy. The sweater fell atop the pile.

"Okay, I've got it," she said of the blanket, but he

hated to let it go. He used it instead to bring her toward him for another kiss, this one deliberate, attentive, exploratory.

She responded with enthusiasm. Her hands inside the quilt were pressed against his chest, and he could tell that she stood on tiptoe. He leaned down to accommodate her while struggling to keep their bodies connected. Holding her in his arms made him feel energized and curiously, inexplicably whole.

He didn't realize until he let go of the blanket, intending to lift her into his arms and place her in the bed, that she'd let go, too. The quilt fell in a colorful puddle at her feet, exposing an exquisite body with small, full breasts, their tips beading with the sudden cold. There was just the smallest curve to her stomach and a subtle fullness in her thighs.

She gasped at the onslaught of cold air. Quickly he carried her to the bed and covered her, then, dispensing with his own clothes, he hurried under the blankets to join her.

THE MOMENT MIKE WRAPPED her in his arms, Colleen lost her resolve to keep her feelings from him. As she stretched languidly against him, a soft sigh of pleasure escaped her lips.

They lay there, flesh to flesh, absorbing each other's warmth. Then Mike's hands began to explore her body, raising gooseflesh on her skin and a thundering in her heart. One moment, his gentle fingertips traced the crenellation of her spine, the curve of her waist, the length of her thigh. The next, his hand cupped her bottom and pressed her to him, the gesture denoting possession.

A thrill rippled along inside her from the hollow of her throat, where his lips settled, to the heart of her womanhood, where a pulse ticked in anticipation.

It occurred to her that there was a lot of passion involved here for "sex with affection," but she was too busily engaged in it to resolve the puzzle.

Mike's hand eased between her thighs, and she opened for him without a second thought. As his fingers teased the sensitive flesh, pleasure began its cat-and-mouse game of approach and retreat.

She was never sure how the game would end. Danny used to say she had a seventy-percent failure rate at reaching sexual fulfillment. But she'd had more tender attention in the last fifteen minutes than she'd had in most of her married…

A wave of pleasure pummeled her with velvet tremors, rattling her from head to toe with the power of its impact. It pinned her to the mattress in stunned paralysis, and as it rode over her again, there was no question who was boss. Love was.

She didn't want it to be—couldn't let it be. She had to seize control.

"You okay, Colleen?" Mike asked. He leaned over her, one hand tracing gentle circles on her stomach. "Why are there tears in your eyes?"

"There aren't." She put a hand up to her face and was surprised when her fingertips came away wet.

He frowned. "Tell me that doesn't mean you're hating it when we've barely gotten started."

She had to smile. "I am not hating it. Would you lie back for me, please?"

He laughed softly but remained on his side. "That was very polite."

"A woman should always be polite when she's about to make love to a man," she said, rising up on her elbow and pushing him onto his back.

"Have sex, you mean," he corrected.

"Shut up," she ordered, and kneeling astride his waist, she braced her hands on his pillow to lean down and plant a kiss on his lips.

He pinched her hip. "Now that was *not* polite."

She bit his lip. "You always have to have the last word."

"The last word? You mean there's finally going to be less talk and more action? Ow!"

That time she bit his ear, then planted a kiss there. She followed with a string of kisses from shoulder to shoulder, then down his chest and abdomen, stopping short of where he clearly awaited her attention.

He tried to sit up, but she pushed him back again with both hands.

"Colleen..." he protested, his voice sounding strangled.

She shushed him. "The kids will hear you." Then she rained kisses down his thigh to his knee, then up again, finally touching him, intending to give him the same pleasure he'd given her.

But he caught her arms, rolled over and tucked her under him, entering her with one swift, urgent thrust.

She couldn't remember ever feeling quite this perfect. There was a moment when they simply looked into each other's eyes, surprised and amazed at this feeling of oneness.

But there was no time to think. He started to move inside her, and as her hips rose to meet his, the tremors came over her again, overwhelming her with sensation.

MIKE CAME BACK TO EARTH with a thud. All the time they'd made love, he'd forgotten that Colleen wasn't his to claim. Holding her, touching her, becoming one with her had been so deliciously right that he had to make himself remember they didn't formally belong to each other.

And that the only way he could hold her was to keep reminding her that he made no claims on her.

But maybe she'd felt the power of that connection the way he had. Maybe it had changed the way she perceived things. Surely she could no longer feel solitary.

She'd wrapped her arms and legs around him, opened her body to him in a way that no mistrusting woman ever could.

He reached over the side of the bed, snagged her sweatshirt and helped her pull it over her head.

''You want the bottoms?'' he asked.

In answer, she pulled him back down to her,

wrapped her arm around his waist and snuggled into his shoulder.

"Just don't say anything," she pleaded in a tight voice that suggested tears. Maybe that feeling of oneness had been only on his part. Or maybe their love-making had been more than she'd expected and she didn't like that. He considered the latter a happy possibility.

"Go to sleep," she grumped.

He had to push just a little. "I thought women hated men who went right to sleep after having sex. Shouldn't we be talking, planning? Whispering endearments?"

She looked up at him, her eyes unhappy. "There's no planning required in a relationship built on affectionate sex."

"Ah." He pretended to accept that. "Okay, then. Good night."

She didn't answer.

CHAPTER TEN

COLLEEN AWOKE TO SUNLIGHT and the rumble of the furnace. She sat up abruptly. The power was back on! Chuie sprawled on the windowsill, happily soaking up the sun.

Power. She looked around at her empty room, empty bed, empty…empty everything. With a groan, she fell back against the pillows.

What had she done?

Made it impossible to believe she could have a casual relationship with Mike Flynn, that's what she'd done. He'd been okay with it, but she'd been shaken to the core, changed on a cellular level. She couldn't do this! What they'd shared had not been sex with affection for the purpose of fun, it had been life-altering lovemaking.

What did she do now? She had no idea.

The door to the next room was open so she leaned out of bed to peer inside and saw that it, too, was empty. Mike and the children must be downstairs having breakfast. The faint waft of tuna close to the floor suggested that the cat had already been fed.

Colleen got laboriously out of bed, noticed with

fresh horror that she was bare-bottomed, though she wore a sweatshirt, and headed for the shower.

She could just decide to trust him, she thought, turning on the taps as she yanked the sweatshirt over her head. She could sweep aside all her old rules and let herself love him. She climbed under the steaming spray of water and took a moment to adjust the temperature. Then she stood directly under the nozzle and let the water beat down on her.

But he hadn't offered love. He'd offered sex.

Still, he'd made love to her. Or had she been the only one aware of the depth of what they'd shared? Perhaps she'd been the only one for whom last night had been a vast emotional experience.

She'd undertaken the experiment in the hope that they would be compatible, that she could accept the terms he offered. That there could be sex and affection in her lonely life without the specter of commitment and permanence threatening her sense of security.

But she'd probably been in love with him since that first night when she had stood with his girls and watched him and her boys walk into the B and B together, looking happy in one another's company. She hadn't wanted to be in love. She'd even convinced herself she could fight it off. But he'd been tender yet possessive in bed, treated her like a queen, held her close afterward and made her feel cherished.

Sometime during the night she'd had a dream of being lost. She was walking the railroad tracks in the dark in a big city, trying to find her bearings, but every landmark she headed for disappeared. Then she'd turned around, sensing danger with a chilling foreboding.

She put a hand to her heart under the beating shower when she remembered that she'd sat up in bed, a scream on her lips.

Mike had sat up beside her. "What?" he'd asked.

After she'd related the dream, he had wrapped his arms around her, pulled her back with him to the pillows, then drawn the covers up over her. He'd held her tightly to him. "The dream of being lost is something we're all familiar with. You usually have it when you're confused about a decision. When I wasn't sure whether to open my own office or go into partnership with Alex Marconeri, I would dream that I was lost in the Guggenheim Museum."

"Why the Guggenheim?" she'd asked.

"Because there are no floors, really," he'd replied. "It's one big spiral from bottom to top. I was looking for a way out, I guess, and there wasn't one. I had to keep walking."

"And you decided to open your own office?"

"Right."

"That was a good decision, wasn't it?"

"I thought so. My wife didn't. Marconeri and Lewin now make a bundle, but I like doing my own thing."

Then he'd made love to her again. They'd taken their time, savoring every new sensation before mov-

ing on to further revelations, then finally came together with the comfort of familiarity as well as passion.

It had been altogether delicious.

But how did she justify that in her life when she
knew they'd never be able to restrict what they felt
to the casual relationship he'd described? She felt too
much and so did he. And she couldn't put her life in
someone else's hands again. She couldn't.

Colleen shampooed her hair, rinsed it off, let the
shower beat on the back of her neck, then turned off
the taps, loath to part from the primitively maternal
embrace of the water. But she couldn't leave her children unattended no matter how willing Mike or their
hosts were to keep an eye out for them.

She pushed the shower curtain back and found herself face-to-face with Mike, who was leaning in the
bathroom doorway.

Her heart melted at the sight of him, then her brain
took over and she remembered that she didn't know
what to do about him. Instinctively she crossed her
hands over her breasts.

He smiled, snatched a towel off the rail and came
to wrap her in it. His lips teased the curve of her neck
and he gave an appreciative sniff. "You smell like
apples."

"It's the shampoo," she breathed, all the emotions
and sensations she'd experienced in his arms last
night returning to further confuse her.

He took a step back and looked worriedly at her

cap of wet hair. "Are you one of those women who require an hour and a half to get ready?"

She laughed. "I have it down to twenty minutes on workdays. Thirty if I have to apply makeup. Why?"

"Do you want to come with me to pick up Tom and Cassandra?"

The last thing she needed was to be confined with him in his van when she had to think things through and decide what to do about their relationship.

"I'd better stay and keep all the kids under..."

"Maureen's got them icing cookies. She's the one who suggested I take you along."

It hadn't been his idea? "You mean you didn't want to otherwise?"

"Of course I did," he replied. "I just thought it'd give the suggestion more weight if you knew she'd made it."

She held the towel close to her, trying to read his mind. Had he felt anything she'd felt last night, or had his touchingly tender treatment of her been her own little fantasy?

"Well...that's not really a sexy and fun endeavor, is it? You're going to rescue two people who've probably had a traumatic night together and will be in need of comfort and tolerance. That's the kind of thing you do with someone who means something to you, who... Ah!"

She gasped as he wrapped an arm around her waist

and lifted her out of the old tub and onto the rug in front of the mirror.

"Please dispense with the stuff that takes extra time," he said. "I'll be back up for you in twenty minutes."

He left without giving her time to argue. She still wasn't entirely sure what he was thinking. That move suggested she meant more to him than sex and fun.

Or he might simply have gotten tired of listening to her.

MIKE DIDN'T KNOW WHAT to think of Colleen's behavior. Last night he'd have sworn he'd made a convert to his belief in love and happiness. Even this morning, when he'd surprised her in the shower, she'd studied him with big-eyed wariness, as though what she believed before last night had been shaken and she wasn't sure what to do about it—or him.

But since he'd helped her into the car and she'd offered a cool and courteous, "Thank you, Michael," he was as unsure of himself as she'd appeared earlier this morning.

First, she'd called him Michael. Even his mother had never used his full name.

He couldn't imagine the purpose of this sudden formality except as a device to keep him at a distance. Colleen chatted politely all the way to Williamstown, laughed at his attempts at humor, felt comfortable enough to change the radio station when the jazz got too hot, but when they passed a tow truck hooking up to a tour bus off the road, she exclaimed, "Michael! Look!"

He glanced quickly in that direction, relieved to see the occupants of the tour bus being helped into various state police vehicles. But he was annoyed at the "Michael" business.

"Annoyed" hardly described the way Cassandra looked when Mike and Colleen drove up. She was waiting in front of room five at the motel, a simple one-story structure that paid homage to colonial architecture with a row of fussy columns supporting the overhang. The parking lot was crowded with cars of travelers probably surprised by the extreme conditions and forced to spend the night.

Cassandra wore Colleen's earmuffs, gloves and mittens, but looked about as warm as the inside of a meat locker.

Tom Crawford paced the length of the building, a cigarette between his fingers.

"Oh-oh," Colleen said as Mike stopped the van.

"Mmm," Mike replied, his eyes on Tom as he wandered toward them, putting his cigarette out in a concrete container nearby. "I'll bet they didn't share the blankets last night."

Cassandra pushed open the sliding door of the van and climbed in, going to the far rear and settling into a corner, her arms folded. "Hi," she said, the civility in her tone obviously an effort. "Thank you for coming for us."

Colleen turned in her seat. "Cassandra, are you okay?"

"Fine," she replied. "Let's just get out of here. Don't bother to wait for Thomas."

Thomas?

Mike felt a kinship with the man, who climbed into the van and settled in behind him with a quiet groan.

"Hey, guys," Tom greeted them. "Glad to see you. Nice of you to come get us."

"Sure," Mike replied. "You had breakfast?"

"Not hungry," Cassandra called from the back.

"Breakfast would be great," Tom countered. "But if you're in a hurry to get back…"

"Actually, we haven't had breakfast, either," Mike said. "I noticed a place as we were coming into town. You mind stopping, Cassandra?" he asked, finding her in the mirror. "You can have a cup of coffee."

"Go ahead," she said. "I'll just wait in the van for you."

Mike turned to Colleen, who raised both eyebrows and buttoned the top button of her jacket as he made a wide turn in the driveway and pulled out onto the road.

In five minutes he was turning into the restaurant's parking lot. Tom opened the sliding door and the aromas of bacon, coffee and warm syrup wafted by. He leapt out, then opened the passenger door for Colleen and helped her out. Mike, walking around the vehicle to join them, stuck his head inside and made one more effort to change Cassandra's mind.

"Whatever you're angry about," he said, "isn't going to be made better or worse by eating breakfast. Why don't you join us?"

She took a whiff of the fragrant air and finally pushed herself out of her seat and jumped gracefully down from the van.

Mike held the door for Colleen and they stepped inside, then Tom held the door for Cassandra, who sailed past him, her chin in the air.

Tom grinned at Mike. "And I left my antacids in the room."

Colleen followed Cassandra to a booth and Mike walked behind with Tom. "I know it isn't my business," he said quietly, "but what the hell happened?"

"She found out I didn't really run out of gas," Tom returned with a level gaze. "The gas gauge was faulty but she thinks I set the whole thing up. She's pretending indignation."

Mike caught a glimpse of Cassandra's stormy expression as she slipped into the far side of the back booth. "It doesn't look like pretense to me."

"Well, I've seen another side of her."

Mike let the subject drop as they reached the booth. Cassandra patted the seat beside her, encouraging Colleen to join her. But Colleen pretended not to see and slipped into the other side. Mike slid in beside her and Tom seemed to square his shoulders before sitting next to Cassandra, who gave him one lethal glance, then concentrated on her menu.

"YOUR AUNTS DON'T LOOK at all the worse for their adventure," Colleen said, eager to make conversation. They were halfway through breakfast and no one had spoken a word except for the courtesies of "pass the pepper, the syrup, the cream…"

Cassandra's features softened just a little. "That's a relief. I was so worried about them."

"And they were worried about you," Colleen went on, cutting a bite of waffle, "when the two of you were missing for so long. Then when Tom called to say you were out of gas in Williamstown…"

Still no one said a word, but Colleen felt a change in the atmosphere. Cassandra stiffened, Tom closed his eyes, and Mike put a hand to her knee as though to shush her.

"You didn't run out of gas?" she asked innocently.

"No," Cassandra said with cool anger. "We didn't. But when Tom stopped, pretending we had, we got broadsided by a taxi that skidded on the ice, and we had to spend the night at a motel." She rolled her eyes. "Running out of gas. How unimaginative is that? And with three little old ladies missing in the sub-zero night."

Tom drew a breath to summon patience, then replied calmly, "I told you that the gauge froze. The mechanic told you that the gauge froze. How difficult is that to understand?"

"It's a lie."

"It's the truth. You just want to believe that every man in this world is after your body. You're so hurt by your fiancé's death that you feel as though you have no soul left. But you're lonely and you want to make contact. So you do everything to make sure the guy sees just the body and not the woman inside.''

Cassandra stared at Tom stoically for a full ten seconds before her eyes pooled with tears and she snatched up her purse, determined to leave. But Tom sat in her path and she had nowhere to go.

Mike began to slide out of the booth, Colleen following, in an attempt to give them privacy. But Tom stopped them. ''No, you two stay and finish your breakfast. I'm going out to have a smoke.''

''You keep smoking,'' Cassandra said, her eyes angry under the tears, ''and you'll have to face some truths about yourself.''

Tom nodded as he dug into a back pocket for his wallet. ''I've been working at it longer than you have,'' he returned quietly. ''I've gained some ground this year, but meeting you hasn't been good for my nerves.''

''Then maybe the running-out-of-gas ploy was a bad idea.''

''It wasn't a ploy,'' he said slowly, succinctly, ''it was the natural result of a cold night and a poor gas gauge. And you're lucky I still had nerves last night, aren't you?''

He put several bills down on the table. ''I'll get breakfast since I ruined it for everyone.''

Mike handed him the keys to the van. ''Go inside

if you get cold.'' He grinned. "But please don't leave without us, okay?"

Tom tossed the keys in his hand and walked away without answering.

When he disappeared, Cassandra put her hands to her eyes and wept.

Colleen reached across the table to touch her arm. "Cassandra, what happened? Did he try to…charm you into something you didn't want last night?"

Cassandra dropped her hands to her lap, the angry hauteur replaced by misery. "No, I tried to 'charm' him, as you so quaintly put it. He turned me down." She shook her head and cried a little harder. "I was embarrassed but thought he was just being gentlemanly, so I…tried a little harder."

"And he gave in?"

Her face crumpled further. "He closed me in the bathroom with all the blankets and my pillow and put a chair in front of the door."

Mike put a hand to his mouth so she wouldn't see the smile if she looked up. Man after his own heart. Sometimes you had to make a point.

"He didn't want to take advantage of you," Colleen offered comfortingly.

Cassandra sniffed and tried to pull herself together. "No," she said grimly. "I think he was just embarrassed by me and didn't want any part of me."

Colleen looked to Mike for help. He hated this kind of thing. Trying to reason with a woman you were involved with was one thing. Reasoning with a woman you didn't really know and who seemed a little high-strung, anyway, was another matter entirely.

But Colleen elbowed him.

"As another man," he said reluctantly, "I don't think that's it."

Cassandra's expression was disbelieving as she crossed her knife and fork over her half-empty plate and pushed it aside. "He's never even noticed me. We just ended up in the same truck because we were looking for my aunts."

"He's noticed you," Mike said with conviction. "You just didn't get the kind of attention from him you wanted. When you tried to force it, the easiest and most immediately gratifying thing for him to do would have been to accept it. But I think he's thinking long term, Cassandra. He didn't want you to regret anything before you get to know each other better."

Lips parted, Cassandra stared at him.

Colleen pushed the other woman's coffee cup toward her. "Here. Have some caffeine. It'll help you think that through." She turned to Mike with respect in her eyes. "That was amazing," she said softly. "And insightful."

He pretended to accept her praise as his due. "Trust me in these things. I'm a doctor."

She barely withheld a smile. "You're a dentist."

"Patients spend a lot of time in the chair, talking to me."

"How can they with all that stuff in their mouths?"

"I've learned to interpret."

When Cassandra had finished her coffee, Colleen looped an arm in hers and led the way toward the counter, where Mike paid the check. Tom paced outside, no cigarette in sight. They resumed their places, Cassandra in the very back, Tom in the middle.

As Mike helped Colleen into her seat, he felt called upon to catch the front of her jacket in his fist and bring her head down for his kiss.

"Mike," she whispered, just before her warm lips met his. Her eyes were turbulent when he released her.

After locking her in, he walked around the van to his side. At least he was no longer "Michael."

CHAPTER ELEVEN

COLLEEN MADE HER DECISION on the silent ride back to Twin Oaks. She wanted an affair with Mike Flynn. The parameters were generally unsatisfactory, but it would keep them in contact, and after just four days in his company, she didn't think she could bear to be completely without him.

In the B and B's parking lot, Tom pushed the side door open and leapt onto the crunchy snow. He opened Colleen's door and helped her down, then turned to close the side door, but Cassandra stood in the opening.

They stared at each other for a moment, her expression still haughty, though subtly softened, his calm but unbending.

"Would you help me down, please?" she asked, reaching for his hand. "I feel sort of…unsteady." A slight tremor in her voice lent truth to her claim.

Suddenly all solicitous, Tom bracketed her waist with his hands and swung her down.

Her face was white. She leaned heavily on one of Tom's arms, and he rubbed a hand in easy circles between her shoulder blades.

"Do you feel faint?" he asked in concern.

"No," she replied, a hand to her stomach. "Just…queasy."

"It's probably from riding in the back of the van," Mike said. "The girls always use the middle seat because the back has a sway to it that makes them nauseous."

"Want to walk a little?" Tom suggested to Cassandra. "Inhale some fresh air and see if you feel better?"

She nodded and they set out across the parking area toward the trees, Tom with an arm around Colleen's shoulders. He turned to shout back, "Thanks again for picking us up!"

Mike waved. "Happy to do it!" He turned to Colleen with a shake of his head. "Now, there's a relationship I wouldn't want to be responsible for working out."

She hooked her arm in his and walked him around the house to the snow-covered lawn in the back, where the children, who were supposed to be icing cookies, were building a snowman instead.

"I thought maybe we could talk about ours," she suggested.

But before he could respond, they were surrounded by her children, his children and the twins. Keegan lifted what appeared to be a snowman torso onto an already established base.

"Mom!" Bugsy said, his eyes glowing, his cheeks and his nose pink. "We're making a snowman family.

All we have so far is the dad, but it's gonna be great!''

"Yeah!'' Angel confirmed. "Maureen has some old clothes we can have and everything. Daddy, we frosted twenty cookies, then we got tired so Maureen said we could come out and play 'cause Keegan's here to watch us.''

Mike and Colleen walked around the snowman and duly admired it, then provided encouragement as Bill and Claudie rolled the head. They applauded as Keegan positioned it atop the torso. He placed an old baseball cap on it and stood Bugsy on a box so that he could press mushrooms in by the stems for eyes. Bugsy leapt down and Angel took his place, applying a carrot nose. Keegan helped the twins set stones in a curve for a smile.

Claudie pointed to the snowman. "That's you, Daddy!''

"The proportions will be about right,'' he laughed, "if I keep eating Clint and Maureen's cooking.''

The finished product admired, the children all pitched in again to roll a base for a new member of the snowman family.

Mike walked Colleen to the far end of the yard, where three oak trees stood on the bank of a small creek.

"What's on your mind?'' he asked as they stopped under one of the trees, its snow-covered branches reaching up to a leaden sky. His manner was calm, but he looked hopeful, she thought.

Colleen was happy that she could please him by giving him what he wanted. "I think an affair's a good idea," she said, hands jammed in her pockets, her lips numbed from the cold. Now that they'd stopped moving, she turned her collar up.

She was surprised that saying the words caused a strange grinding sensation in the middle of her chest. She knew the problem, but she was getting what she wanted—or what she used to want. And he was getting what he wanted. So why was there a problem? She ignored her doubts and made herself go on.

"And the way you've laid it out should work well. We'll keep the kids out of it, and meet…what? Once a week?"

His dark blue gaze, the color of dusk on a stormy day, held hers for a moment. And in the heart of it, she saw disappointment. Bitter disappointment. It surprised her out of her slouch against the tree.

He turned his gaze up to the sky, where dark clouds hung heavily. When he looked down at her again and smiled, she'd have sworn she was mistaken about what she'd seen.

"Good," he said. "That's great, Colleen."

Now she heard the disappointment in his voice, despite the covering smile he offered. She was filled with the sense that things were wrong, out of place, definitely out of tune.

She felt her own smile crumple and saw him notice it. He reached an arm out to bring her to him.

"What is it?" she asked, blocking his gesture with

her own arm. "You *don't* think it's good or great, no matter what you say. I can see it in your eyes. They're always honest, and you're not happy." A horrible thought occurred to her. "You didn't enjoy the love-making," she guessed. "And you're too polite to say so."

"That's completely ridiculous," he denied instantly, catching her hand. "I can't believe you even said it." Then he pulled her to him to kiss her long and soundly. "I am crazy about you and we're going to have great fun together."

"Then, why do you look upset?"

"I'm not upset."

"What are you?"

"Caught off guard, I guess."

"But it was your plan. Why would you have to be *on* guard about it? If you didn't think we were compatible last night, you can tell me. I'm an adult."

He caught her in one arm and covered her mouth playfully with his other hand. "If you say that one more time, I'm going to wash your mouth out with soap."

"I just thought…" she began, when he lifted his hand.

He cut her words off by covering her mouth again. "Don't think. Just listen to what I'm telling you and believe it."

She wanted to say "I know you're lying," but he replaced his hand with his lips and she lost her chance.

He led her back toward the house, telling her she looked pinched and cold. She felt that way inside. All the words seemed wrong. *Crazy* about her. *Fun. Once a week.* Still, she told herself, it was better than nothing.

Was that all life should be about? she wondered. Better than nothing?

SMART GUY, MIKE TOLD HIMSELF. He was about to get what he wanted. He'd be able to continue to see Colleen without her feeling threatened by love and all its little hooks. He'd have been happy to be hooked by her, but he'd take what he could get.

He had to take better care that she didn't see in his eyes how disappointed he was that they couldn't share something more. Her misinterpretation of his disappointment would have been ludicrous if he didn't feel so guilty that she could even think something like that.

Chewie pulled on his lead, happy to be out for this walk. Mike felt the same way. No children to claim his attention. No woman to confuse his thinking.

As he walked, he took stock of his life. He knew it was a mistake—at least emotionally—but he kept feeling unsure of his position and he hated that. He liked to know where he stood—even if it was under forty pounds of manure.

His dentistry practice was thriving. That was good. He had two daughters he adored, though he saw them far less often than he wanted. Having them was wonderful, seeing them so seldom was not.

Now he also had a friendship with two young boys he felt very fond of and who seemed to like him. That was very good. He was about to embark on an affair with the boys' mother, which was wonderful on one level, but only passably good on another. He'd get to see her, but without the permanence to their relationship he really wanted.

To sum up, he thought as Chewbacca walked sedately down the road, his professional life was good, but his personal life stood directly under that manure pile.

He had to do something about it.

His cell phone rang and he fished it out of his pocket, wondering who it could be. His office was closed.

"Hello," he said, stopping as Chewie analyzed a bush.

"Mike?" It was Marianne. She sounded breathless.

Somehow he'd forgotten to list his ex-wife in the less-than-wonderful aspects of his life.

"Yeah," he replied. "What's up?"

"Thank God!" she exclaimed. "I was so afraid you'd be out of reach or something. I mean, I know that you're sort of on vacation."

So far it had been curious as vacations went, but certainly life-altering. "Yes. And so are you. How's Provincetown?"

"Wonderful!" she exclaimed. "In fact, that's why I'm calling."

"Really." He couldn't imagine where this was going. He sat down on a tree stump and waited for her to go on.

"Nardo's patron came to see him at the gallery, and he says his work is so wonderful he's sending him to Madrid to study with Catalano, something Nardo's wanted to do for years!"

She said it as though it was something momentous. "Who's Catalano?" he asked.

"Only the greatest naive folk surrealist working today!" she declared.

Okay, it *was* momentous. When they'd been married, Marianne hadn't known an impressionist painting from an etching.

He wasn't sure what to say. *Get him to clean up the driveway before he goes?*

Then an awful thought occurred to him. And she seemed to pick it right out of his brain when she said quietly, significantly, "Nardo says he can't go without his muse."

Oh, God.

"Mike, I'm going to Madrid!" She squealed her delight. "Can you believe it? And we're going to live part of the time in the city and part of the time on Tenerife, where Catalano has another place. He's a major eccentric, I guess, and paints in a toga."

He couldn't breathe. He rose to his feet, anger rising up in him like a geyser. He opened his mouth to tell her if she thought she was taking his girls almost six thousand miles away from him, she should have her head examined; when she said in that small wheedling voice, "Oh, Mike, I know it's such short notice, but please tell me you can take custody of the girls! We'll be there for a couple of years, and while in some ways it'd be good for them to be abroad, in other more practical ways, it'll be too disruptive. And they live for their visits with you. I don't think they'd do well so far from you. They can come and see us for a couple of weeks in the summer and maybe Christmas."

Blood rushed back to his brain. A world turned inside out suddenly shook itself right again. She was finally abdicating motherhood for the sake of a man. He could have custody! He had to clear his throat.

"Yes, of course I'll take custody. When are you leaving?"

"Next week. When you bring the girls home, I'd like to keep them a couple of days, get all their things packed, have time to explain this to them and say goodbye."

"Sure."

"What'll you do about Chewie? I know your condo won't let you have him."

He was thinking fast. "I'll start looking for a house," he said. "I'll think of something. Marianne, you're that sure about Nardo?" With lives being turned upside down all around, he felt obliged to ask.

She didn't even hesitate. "He requires nothing of me except a body to paint and make love with."

"And that's all right with you?" He didn't quite get it.

"Of course." She sighed. "I don't seem to be able to find a man with the money that would make me happy, so the next best thing is a man willing to make me the focal point of his work, so that I don't have to compete for his attention."

He had to appreciate her honesty if not her life philosophy.

"Then, I hope you'll be happy."

"I know you will. Will you tell the girls so they'll be prepared?"

"Don't you want to do that?"

There was a moment's hesitation, then she said with a trace of guilt, "You know how I am about the hard stuff."

Yes. He did. "All right. I'll take care of it."

"Thank you, Mike."

"Sure. See you Sunday."

"Bye."

Chewie bounded toward him, tail wagging, ready to continue their walk. Mike was half tempted to head back to the girls with the news, but he needed a moment to absorb the information, to accept the change this would make in his life.

After two long years, he was finally going to have what he wanted—custody of his children, family life. He felt like a man walking from shadow into sunlight.

And this changed the stakes with Colleen. If he could have his children, he might as well go for broke.

Chewie pulled on the leash, urging him on. He followed, arm stretched out ahead of him as the large dog towed him. Dealing with Colleen was not going to be easy, he accepted fatalistically. But he was determined to have her.

THE GIRLS WERE LESS THAN enthusiastic about being taken away from their snowman construction. Chewie, however, was ecstatic at having his walk extended.

"I just want to talk to you for a few minutes," he said as he caught Angel's hand and drew her along with him across the parking area and into the woods. Claudie followed, kicking at the snow.

"We were having so much fun," she said moodily. "I like Bill and Bugsy. I hope we can still play with them after we go home. New Bedford's not too far from Boston, is it?"

"Only fifty miles," he replied. Then added to himself, *And I have plans to remove the distance altogether.*

"What do we have to talk about?" Claudie asked, coming up beside him. "We're not in trouble, are we?"

"No," he assured her quickly. "It's just that I got a call from your mom this morning."

Claudie stopped in her tracks, her eyes wide and stricken. "Do we have to go back early?"

Mike kept moving and gestured her to follow. "No. But your mom and I both wondered how you'd feel about living with me."

Claudie remained in place for a moment, then ran to catch up. "You mean, *all* the time?"

It was impossible to tell if her question suggested happiness or dismay.

He held his breath. "*All* the time."

She smiled quickly. "Well, yeah." Then she frowned. "But, how come?"

He explained about Nardo's news.

"It's not that Mom doesn't love you more than anything, she just…"

Claudie nodded. "Needs a boyfriend. I know."

He was stunned by that perception.

"She's probably like Bill and Bugsy's father."

"How's that?"

"Bill said he's just not family material." She delivered the words with a philosophical shrug. He was forever amazed by what children understood. Though Colleen had undoubtedly used those words with Bill, he'd grasped their meaning enough to pass on the information to Claudie. "He didn't like doing the hard stuff, just like Mom. You always have to take us to the doctor, or talk to our teachers, or tell us when we're not going to get something we want. That stuff."

If anything ever made him sympathetic to Marianne, it was the fact that she had contributed to making this amazing child and her sister.

"So, you're okay with it?" he asked.

Claudie smiled widely. "I'm really happy. Living with you always feels more real."

"Real." He wasn't sure what that meant.

"Yeah. You know we're there. There isn't somebody else in the house more important to you than we are."

He leaned down to hug her while Angel scooped up snow in a mittened hand.

"What about school?" she asked.

"I'm in a different district," he answered, "but you can finish out the year where you are, then we'll see about next year. You already know some of the kids in my neighborhood. You might like going to school with them."

She nodded. "I know kids change schools all the time. I just think it's a little scary."

"Well, we'll work it out when the time comes." As Angel skipped on ahead, ignoring them, he called her back. "Angel, do you want to live with me?" he asked.

She squinted, collecting more snow. "I thought we already did."

When he looked surprised, Claudie explained knowingly, "I know what she means. Even though we spend more days at Mom's, it's really like we live with you and visit her, you know?"

Live with you and visit her. If he wondered how

they felt about him as a father, there it was. But he wanted to make sure Angel understood.

"You won't get to visit Mom," he explained, "until the summer."

She formed the snow in her hand into a ball. "Okay," she said with a gleeful giggle, and threw it at him.

THAT HURDLE PAINLESSLY cleared, he prepared to take on Colleen. He found her at the desk in her room, one hand in her hair while she crossed out something she'd written on a piece of paper. Fu Manchu sat on the back of the desk, batting at the top of her pen. That was the most activity he'd seen from the cat since they'd arrived.

The door was open and he took a step inside, a steaming mocha in each hand, getting a whiff of Colleen's floral fragrance from across the room.

She looked up, wariness stealing into her concentration as she focused on him. "Hi," she said. She tapped the small pile of paper on her desk with a pen. "I'm trying to do the welcome for Father Gallagher."

"Are you feeling inspired?"

She laughed mirthlessly. "I'm feeling stressed. I have to have it finished tomorrow. Mercifully, Clint said he could set the type for me on the computer and it'll look like I did it with pen and ink. Why? Did you come to help?"

He walked into the room, offered her the mocha topped with whipped cream and sat on the foot of the bed with the plain one. "No poetic skill, I'm afraid. But I wanted to offer help of a different kind. Can you take a brief break?"

With a smile, she turned in her chair so that she faced him. "I'd hate to risk you walking away with the mocha if I said no. Where'd you get them, anyway?"

"Clint was making them for him and Maureen."

"Yum. Okay." She sipped at the cup, wiped whipped cream from her lip with a swipe of her index finger, then licked her finger. He lost focus for a minute. "I hope you're going to tell me what was really in your eyes when I told you I wanted the affair."

"Can you handle the truth?" he asked calmly. He didn't feel calm at all. He stood to lose everything.

She sat up straighter. "We're not going to play the Tom Cruise-Jack Nicholson scene from *A Few Good Men*, are we?"

He took a deep slug of the hot, caffeine-laden drink, propped a foot on the edge of her chair and looked straight into her eyes.

"You were right this morning," he said directly, praying he wasn't making a mistake. "When you told me you were okay with an affair, I was disappointed." Her eyes widened and she seemed to lift off the chair, so he shook his head quickly. "Not with you or your acceptance, but with what I had to settle for."

Now she appeared confused as well as upset. "What do you mean?"

"Sex with affection instead of love."

"But you're the one…"

"I know. I made the proposition because I didn't want to lose you, and that was all you were willing to let me have."

She looked guilty.

He approached this part carefully. "But, if I'm reading you correctly, it's not really enough for you anymore, is it?"

She gave a little gasp, then fiddled nervously with her cup, putting it down, picking it up, then down again.

"We made love," he said quietly. "We didn't have sex with affection. If that was affection, then our love could melt the polar ice cap."

This time her eyes were turbulent with emotions Mike couldn't begin to interpret.

PANIC AND EXCITEMENT jolted Colleen in equal measure. He did want more! But now that she faced the possibility of having it, she wondered if she was capable of giving it.

"The affair," she said in a gravelly voice, "would have been tidy and…" She cleared her throat. "Easy."

He rested his elbows on his knees and leaned toward her. "Colleen, the stakes are changing for me. I'm getting custody of the girls."

"What?"

"Marianne called me this morning while I was out

walking Chewie.'' He explained about Nardo and the patron.

"I just talked to the girls and they're happy."

She smiled, thrilled for him. "Of course they are. They adore you."

"They like your boys," he went on. "And they think you're wonderful. So—since I'm finally getting what I've wanted so desperately, I thought I may as well go after everything I want. Don't you think we should chuck this whole affair idiocy and go for the real thing?"

Her lungs felt as if they were collapsing. "Real…thing?" she asked in a strangled voice.

"Real," he repeated firmly. "Love. Marriage. Family. Everything there is when two people love each other."

She could not have explained to anyone how much she wanted the same things—or how afraid she was to concede anything to gain them. She opened her mouth to speak, but no sound came.

He was watching her worriedly. "Okay, think about this," he said. "If you marry me, you can be home for the kids like you've always wanted to be. I'm not rich, but we're very comfortable. We'll sell the condo and buy a house where you can have that studio you've always dreamed about. Maybe a room upstairs with a bay window and a wonderful view, north light, lots of open floor space.

"We'll make sure there are a couple of guest bedrooms so your sister can come and visit." He shrugged, smiling tauntingly. "We could have more kids. And if you're serious about retiring in New England, we could think about living in Cooper's Corner in our old age."

She remained speechless.

"Say something," he pleaded.

A *yes* answer wasn't possible. She was the bad-luck girl. It would be like building her life on papier-mâché. It would look good but it couldn't possibly stand up over time. Could it?

But a *no* answer was unthinkable.

"I know how you hate sharing control over your life with anyone," he coaxed, "but I promise I'd make no demands on you except that you be there."

And that, he didn't seem to understand, was the big one.

Still, when she looked into his denim-blue eyes, all the things that worried her seemed to dissolve into nothingness. She considered the last four and a half days, and she couldn't remember when she'd had more fun, felt safer, more comfortable. He treated her boys with greater care than their father ever had. Even given her past experience with men, she'd be hard put to confuse him with her father or her ex-husband.

Mike Flynn was a genuine original.

Maybe it was time she showed some guts, took a chance.

"Yes!" she said. Her whole being suddenly sparkled with the decision. Every nerve ending prickled.

He blinked. "Pardon me?"

"Yes!" she said, taking his mocha from him and putting it beside hers on the desk. "Yes. Yes, I'll marry you."

"Well, I'll be damned," he said as he caught her to him and fell back onto the mattress. "I was sure you'd have to think about it."

"I don't. I know you're wonderful. I know we're wonderful together. What is there to think about?"

He tucked her close to him and turned them until he was uppermost. "Why, Colleen O'Connor," he said, his eyes roving her face with concentration. "I do believe you've finally come to your senses."

"That might be assuming too much. But you may kiss me, anyway."

He did, and she was even further convinced that they would be deliriously happy together, that she had nothing to fear from the past.

Propping himself up on an elbow, he studied her as though he found her endlessly fascinating.

"I suppose the noble thing to do would be to track down the children and tell them, rather than making love and letting Maureen watch them as she does with such style."

She sighed, her fingertip tracing the line of his chin. "I'm afraid so. Except for the telling them part. We should wait for a quieter moment. And your girls have already had something big to deal with today."

A faint line furrowed his eyebrows. "I don't hear a trace of doubt in your voice, do I?"

"No," she replied. It was oddly unsettling to say

it. As though she lied. That thought so startled her that she said even louder, "No! Why? Are you having second thoughts?"

His frown deepened fractionally. "No. I guess I'm just a little worried about your sudden and complete about-face."

"Maybe you're more convincing than you realize."

The cat leapt from the desk to the bed and wedged its way between them, purring.

"I'd like to think that's it." He seemed to want to, but his eyes traveled over her face, trying to read behind her smile. He stroked the cat, who nuzzled his chin. "Miracles abound today."

She did her utmost to make her smile brighter, but felt it tighten instead.

There was a light rap on the door. "Colleen?" It was Maureen's voice. "Is Mike with you?"

"Are you?" she asked Mike softly. "Or are you against me?"

"Oh, I'm with you." He pushed himself up and went to the door.

"Oh, hi," Maureen said. "Cooper's Corner Automotive is here with Colleen's car."

"Thanks," he said. "Would you tell them I'll be right down, please?"

"Sure." She smiled innocently. "Don't hurry. I gave him coffee and a shamrock cookie."

Mike went through the door that connected their

rooms and emerged with his wallet. "I'll be right back," he said. "Don't forget where we were."

Jeez. How badly did she have it, she asked herself, if she'd almost forgotten she had a car?

CHAPTER TWELVE

WILBUR CALHOUN FOLLOWED Mike out into the B and B's parking lot, still munching on a green cookie. "Pretty well-maintained little car," he said as Mike stopped several feet away to study the new door. It looked better than the original, actually. No parking lot scratches or gouges from the key. The silver-gray paint was a perfect match. "But its days are numbered. These little imports will go on forever, but when I serviced it like you asked, I noticed that the trunk leaks and I spotted rust in a few places. At least it'll look good until it goes."

Mike opened and closed the door. It worked smoothly.

"Thanks, Wilbur," he said, stepping back to shake the mechanic's hand. "I appreciate it. What do I owe you?"

Wilbur handed him the bill.

Mike had propped his checkbook against the trunk to write the check when a woman's voice shouted, "Stop!"

He knew without turning who the voice belonged

to, and he heard an undercurrent in it that meant trouble. He'd thought his proposal had gone too smoothly.

Reluctantly Mike made himself turn to face Colleen. He couldn't imagine what had happened to her in the five minutes since he'd been in her company, but her eyes were red and there was an unholy light in them.

"I have to pay Wilbur," he said calmly, trying to ward off a scene.

"No, you don't," she said, coming to stand between them and smiling at the mechanic. "Hi, Wilbur. I'm Colleen O'Connor. This is my car. Mr. Flynn had it repaired without my consent."

"Colleen…" Mike began.

"That doesn't mean I don't intend to pay you," she went on, running a hand over the new door. "You did a beautiful job. But I wondered if we could work something out."

Wilbur looked as though he was going to have trouble digesting the cookie.

"How much is it?" Colleen persisted. She spotted the bill in Mike's hand and snatched it from him.

When she saw the amount, she paled and might have reeled backward, but Mike had taken hold of her arm.

He smiled at Wilbur, who looked worried. "Would you excuse us a minute, please?" Mike asked, and before waiting for an answer, tugged Colleen with him closer to the house.

"What are you doing?" he asked, not sure he wanted to know.

"I'm taking care of my own debts," she said stubbornly, staring at him with her mouth firmed and her chin angled, as though she expected trouble from him.

"I thought we were getting married."

"What does that have to do with anything?"

He couldn't quite believe the question. "A lot," he replied calmly. "We share things, for one."

"This isn't sharing. The money's all yours." She raised a hand for silence when he would have objected. "And it occurred to me just now as I was standing upstairs, thrilled that my car had been repaired and it wasn't going to take me thirty-six months of costly payments, that I can't marry you."

He'd known that was coming. Cussed woman. What he didn't understand was why. She seemed determined to tell him.

"You take things over for me and I object and spit fire, but deep down, I like the fact that you relieve me of the responsibility. I struggled to see that Jerri and I had what we needed since I was nine, even bargaining with the pharmacist to baby-sit for her an entire weekend so I could pay for Jerri's inhaler. With my own children, the needs are more frequent and more immediate and I have to find a way to meet every one. So I appreciate what a gift it is that you're willing to take care of me."

"I'm not..." he began, but she hadn't finished.

"I was coming down to look at the car," she continued, "feeling happy but with a nagging sense that something was wrong about the situation. And then I realized what it was."

He didn't want to hear it.

"If I let you pay for taking care of my car," she said, her eyes unhappy, her voice thin, "and marry you and let you give me a studio and do all the things for me that I've dreamed of all along, I'll be no better than Danny was."

"What?" He couldn't help the scornful disbelief. "That's absurd!"

"That's how I feel."

"Then you're just looking for a way out, and you're trying to find something else to blame besides the fact that you're too tight-fisted with your trust to share life with somebody else." He was surprised at how quickly and angrily that came out. He'd now moved from disbelieving to furious.

She withstood the blast, her stance becoming more rigid. Back at the car, Wilbur shifted uncomfortably, obviously trying to make himself invisible.

"This man did great work in record time," Mike said, nodding his head toward Wilbur.

"I fully intend to pay him," she retorted hotly, "just…not this instant. I can give him fifty dollars and…fifty dollars a month until it's paid."

"I'm paying him now," Mike said. "If you're going to get silly about the bill…"

"It's my car!"

"I ordered the repair!"

"Well, maybe you shouldn't take things upon yourself that aren't your concern."

He counted to ten. He managed to lower his voice, if not the level of his anger. "You're telling me you're not my concern?"

"That's exactly what I'm telling you!" she retorted, standing on tiptoe to get right in his face. "You will not take over my problems because you're bigger and have more money."

"That's not why I tried to do it and you know it. You don't want me to because you're afraid of being indebted—afraid that means you'll have to somehow return the favor."

She arched an eyebrow, intending to give his suggestion a salacious quality.

He scolded her with a look. "Don't try to make it sound as though you're protecting your virtue from me, when all you're really trying to do is protect your little monarchy. You couldn't depend on anyone in the past so now you're going to be an island. An atoll. You know the difference between an island and an atoll?"

Her eyes lost focus as she thought.

"An atoll is rocky," he said. "Hardly anything grows on it!"

He didn't give her a chance to reply. "Now, I'm paying Wilbur because he did the work I asked him to do. If you insist on taking care of it yourself, we'll work that out later."

He expected her to storm away. He was a little

surprised when she simply followed him to the car, where he wrote out the check and handed it to Wilbur.

With a quick thank-you, the mechanic shrugged apologetically at Colleen, then climbed into his truck and squealed down the long driveway.

Colleen was waiting for him, hands on her hips, when he turned around. The reality of what this argument meant was beginning to sink in, and what little patience he'd managed to hang on to dissolved like sugar in boiling water.

"Good thing we didn't book a church," he said.

She looked at him as though he'd cut the ground out from under her.

"How could you simply dismiss my wishes like that?" she demanded.

"Because it wasn't logical, Colleen. I ordered the work done because I wanted to help you and because, however inadvertently, it was partly my fault. Don't you see what you're doing?"

"Trying to protect my autonomy?" she asked, sarcasm masking as innocence.

"Bull. A big word that means 'alone.'" He was pacing now, needing to expend the energy accelerating inside him. "You complain that there's never been a man in your life you could trust, then one comes along who tries to prove he can be counted on, and you're offended. What kind of sense does that make?"

"God, Mike, isn't there some middle ground between abandonment and assumption of control? You can't have things the way you want them just because you want them.''

"And neither can you. If you want me in your life, you can't relegate me to a storage locker until you need a bed partner or someone to shoot hoops with the boys. I was brought up to look after my family.''

She put both hands to her face, obviously as exasperated as he felt. Then she lowered them, and he saw that it was more than that. She had a complete lack of understanding of his position—just as he had of hers.

FOR TWO CENTS, COLLEEN WOULD have packed up the boys and headed for New Bedford tonight. But they'd all committed themselves to Father Gallagher's celebration, and a promise was a promise. She had a welcome banner to finish and her children and Mike's had their duties as leprechauns to perform.

Some pot of gold.

"I think it's pretty clear we're over,'' she said stoically. She felt as though someone had finally come along with that skillet.

"Pretty clear,'' he agreed.

"We'll have to be civil to each other because of the children and Father Gallagher.''

"I'm sure we can do that.''

She turned away before he could see tears well in her eyes, and the first thing she spotted at the end of the back lawn were the children's snow people. The base for the second snowman had become a female, obviously a mother figure with an old purse hanging on a branch that protruded from her side. Standing beside her were two snow children, also female, wearing the hats and scarves Mike had bought for his daughters the day before.

On the other side of the parental pair were two more snow children, these male, one with obvious attitude, the other wearing one of Bugsy's many Bugs Bunny sweatshirts.

It was all of them, the Flynns and the O'Connors, as a family.

And right beside them, apparently having heard everything, stood Bill and Bugsy, Claudie and Angel. Each little face glowered up at her. They'd clearly put their wishes for the future into the snow family.

Unable to explain to them what had just happened when she didn't understand it herself, Colleen ran for the house.

COLLEEN, MAUREEN AND Cassandra all went to the church early Friday afternoon to help in the kitchen.

Tom had received word that morning that he'd been hired by the town of Cooper's Corner, and Mike had noticed that he and Cassandra, who'd remained at the B and B after her aunts left, had been having some deep discussions while curled up together in front of the fire.

It was nice to know, he thought, that romance was in bloom for someone.

Today the promise of spring was in the air. The

sun was high, the snow was melting, and there was something else, the suggestion of change. As he walked Chewie in the backyard while the children made a desultory effort to strengthen their snow family against the sun, Mike wondered if it was only that he knew his own life would never be the same.

He took a deep gulp of air and remembered Colleen asking him if he could smell snow coming. He'd admitted that he couldn't, but he wondered if he might be able to now. Every sense and nerve ending he possessed seemed honed to a finer point than it had been when he'd arrived. Love, he thought, punctuates every awareness with an exclamation mark.

He tried to imagine what his life would be like when he got home with the girls. He would have to find a house, readjust his schedule, hire a nanny. Life would be frantic for a while, but they would adjust. There would still be a large emptiness where Colleen and her boys should have been.

When he walked back toward the children, he found them kicking the snow family apart.

''It was melting,'' Bill said, his face grim, his eyes troubled. ''We couldn't stop it.''

''Yeah.'' Claudie kicked at the bottom of the snow person that represented her. It broke in half and snow went flying. ''A lot of kids don't have two parents.''

She turned to the figure that represented Colleen. Its expression had changed from that of a cheerful mom to one of uncertainty as the head melted toward the shoulder in a lopsided shrug. He sighed. How appropriate.

Claudie took the purse off the stick that represented an arm, then reared back as though to give the snow-woman a kick. Bill and Bugsy looked as if they were going to take it personally.

Then his daughter simply sat down in the snow, apparently unable to harm the image of Colleen. The other children collected around her, understanding her feelings.

Mike walked into the middle of them and hunkered down to their height. Chewie gave every face a slurp, then plopped down on the ground.

Claudie leaned against Mike's arm. "I thought…I mean, it looked like…we were all going to stay together."

Bill wrapped an arm around Mike's neck. "I wanted to go home with you."

Mike hugged them. "I know. We all think we should get to have things the way we want them, but sometimes that's not best for us. God has a plan and we just have to trust that he knows what he's doing."

"Yeah." Bill sighed and leaned his weight against him. "You only get what you want fifty percent of the time. That's what Mom says."

"That's about right. Maybe even generous, sometimes."

"She said she was a hundred percent happy, though, 'cause she had me and Bugsy." Bill sighed.

"I bet that won't be true anymore, though. 'Cause she really liked you. And Claudie and Angel."

He held the boy closer. "I know. I've come to love you guys, too."

"Daddy," Claudie said, her voice thick with tears. "Can't you fix it?"

"No, I can't. We just have to accept that Colleen wants to be independent. Everyone has a right to do what they want to do with their life. It's a free country. The Minuteman died for that, remember? We all have to do what we think is best for us."

"That sucks," Bill said emphatically.

"Big time," Mike had to agree.

CHAPTER THIRTEEN

"PEACE TO ALL WHO ENTER HERE, and the luck of the wee folk to you. May love be yours from morn to eve, and guide you in all you do."

The children rushed into the church hall without noticing the welcome rhyme Colleen had created. Mike was torn between following the children and needing to read the rhyme again.

"We'll keep an eye on them," Clint said as he and Tom Crawford went inside. Then Clint stuck his head out again. "But don't be long. We're setting up tables and chairs."

"Be...right there," Mike said absently, his attention on the sign as he read it again. Someone, he thought, should practice what she preached.

COLLEEN, DRIVEN BY GUILT, misery and total confusion, outperformed everyone on the decorating committee. She strung crepe paper from the very top of a high ladder while Maureen and Cassandra shouted cautions along with instructions. She hung balloons and green foil shamrocks on strings dangling from the high ceiling.

"We use the strings every year," Father Gallagher said as he walked by with a case of soft drinks. "At Christmas we hang paper snowflakes, at Easter it's lilies and tulips, in the summer, American flags. Mrs. O'Connor, you're making me nervous up there. And why is the shortest woman on the ladder?"

"Because she seems to have a death wish this afternoon, Father," Maureen replied. "But we're watching her, don't worry."

He moved doubtfully toward the kitchen, his eye on Colleen, who was reaching forward to hang a cluster of balloons. "All right, but I'm going to be busy in the kitchen and I don't want to be called out here to perform last rites."

Colleen blew him a kiss.

"Incidentally, Mrs. O'Connor..."

"Yes, Father?"

"Lovely welcome scroll."

"Thank you."

The men and the children had arrived and everyone was helping to set up tables and chairs for the dinner.

The children greeted Colleen in an unusually subdued manner. Her boys were angry at her for her quarrel with Mike, and though the girls were less hostile about it, it was clear they were also upset.

She understood their dismay. She'd wanted it to work out, too, but a woman couldn't give up her personal beliefs to satisfy a man's vision of how things should be—particularly if that involved giving her everything and doing everything for her.

She'd tried to explain that to Maureen and Cassandra when they found her crying in the tiny, two-stalled ladies' room.

Maureen seemed to understand, but Cassandra made no pretense of her own confusion. "He bought you a scarf you claim you didn't need, had your car repaired and paid for it for you, and wants to marry you and bring your two boys into his family, even though he's getting custody of his two girls."

Colleen closed her eyes as Cassandra ran through her list of grievances. At face value it sounded...

"Crazy!" Cassandra said with no consideration for Colleen's feelings. Colleen noticed absently that Cassandra looked gorgeous in a dark green dress. "You're upset with Mike because he wants to do everything for you, including love your children? What is the *matter* with you?"

"I don't want him to take over my life!" Colleen explained defensively.

"He's doing the things for you that you can't do for yourself—at least without a lot of self-sacrifice. And being a father to the boys is something you could never do."

"She's just feeling a little self-protective," Maureen placated, putting an arm around Colleen's shoulder. "When you've been on your own for a while, you put up some defenses. It's only normal. I can understand that."

Cassandra nodded. "So can I. I did it myself. But the time comes when you have to look fear in the face and spit." She grinned. "Not very ladylike, I know, but when you're fighting for your happiness, you have to get tough. Colleen, do you really want to struggle the rest of your life without someone beside you?"

She could have said no to that without consideration, but she would never give up the strength she'd acquired through independence. "I know I can cope by myself if I have to."

"Okay, that's it right there," Cassandra said, pointing a finger in her face. "You can cope by yourself. Great. It's wonderful to know that. But do you have to keep doing it just to prove to yourself that you can, when there's a wonderful man who wants to share his life with you and your children?"

Colleen thought about that, felt herself vacillate over her conviction that she wanted to take care of her family by herself.

"It's strengthening to know you can be self-sufficient and self-contained," Cassandra pressed, drawing her hands in close to her chest. "But you can't love that way. Love requires that you reach out." She spread her arms, then hugged Colleen. "You did that for me when I was closed in my room and worried about my aunts and wanting to talk to somebody but afraid it would show my weaknesses. You kept trying to make me share, inviting me downstairs for coffee." She sighed, shaking her head. "I closed the door in your face, as I recall. Then I got in a truck with Tom Crawford and completely lost all desire to remain isolated. I went about it the wrong way in the beginning, but I finally got it right.''

Cassandra smiled a young, girlish smile. ''He's moving to Cooper's Corner in two weeks to start his job. I'm closing up my office and relocating here.''

Colleen hugged her, delighted that things had worked out for Cassandra and Tom.

Maureen glanced at her watch. ''Okay, you two, we're going to be swarmed with hungry parishioners in about ten minutes.'' She gave her hair a pat, then led the way back to their posts in the kitchen.

MIKE TRIED TO BUM a cigarette from Tom, who stood outside while everyone ate. Inside, the lights were low, the tables covered with green linen cloths and candlelight. Cheerful conversation created a low buzz, punctuated by laughter and friendly shouts that filtered out the partially open door. Bill, Bugsy, Claudie, Angel and several children of the parish circulated in leprechaun garb pouring water, taking orders for beverages other than coffee, and delivering them to the tables.

Outside the night was cold but clear, stars glittering in a random pattern.

''Don't have a pack in my pocket,'' Tom said with a regretful grin at Mike. ''Didn't know you smoked.''

Mike leaned both hands on the back of a bench that faced the church's small, fenced graveyard, which was filled with the families that founded the parish in the middle of the last century.

"It's been about six years. I accidentally burned Claudie with the lit tip of one when she was a toddler. It was just superficial, but I felt so bad about it, I quit. But I feel as though I need something. And a cigarette seemed safer than alcohol since I'm driving us home."

Tom nodded empathetically. "Women. Gotcha. The kids told me they thought you guys were all going home together, then Colleen...what? Got scared?"

Mike nodded. "I think so. I understand—sort of. We've only known each other a week and what we have feels big. It would scare me, except that it's what I've always wanted. I'm a lousy bachelor."

"You haven't given up on her, have you?"

"No." Mike sighed. "I'm planning strategy."

"Strategy!" Father Gallagher appeared behind them, a bottle in one hand, three plastic glasses in the other. "Are we going to war, gentlemen?"

He put the glasses down on the bench and began to pour. "It's only sparkling apple cider," he said, handing a glass to Tom. "Wanted you to know how much I appreciate your efforts for us, you not even being parishioners. It was good of you to help."

He poured a drink for Mike, then one for himself.

"Shall we toast strategy?" he asked, holding up his glass. "Has the dinner gotten so rowdy it's time to fix bayonets? Catholics do get loud, you know."

"Strategy for our ongoing war with women," Mike clarified, touching glasses with Tom and the priest.

"Ah. The battle of the sexes." The priest took his place between them, looking up at the stars. "That's one I don't know much about in detail, except that I think everyone has it wrong."

"In what way?" Tom asked.

"Well." The priest gestured with his glass, then looked from one man to the other. "Everyone thinks love is a matter of the heart, but it isn't."

"It isn't?"

"No. Though I have no personal experience, I've counseled many a couple in my time, and I'm telling you that love can't be trusted to the heart. The heart attracts you to each other, but then it gets hurt, gets jealous, gets angry. It's the head that realizes life is a long, lonely journey, and without someone to lean on, and someone to lean on you, it's a harder, duller trip. The heart may draw you together, but it's the head that keeps you together." He turned to Mike. "Witness the fact that you were just planning strategy. That's a thinking man's approach to love. I'd say you're destined for success."

"Can you get me a guarantee on that, Father?" Mike teased.

Father Gallagher looked up at the dark sky. "He's asking for a guarantee on that, Heavenly Father."

And then, so quickly Mike wasn't sure he saw it until he heard Tom's disbelieving gasp and felt the priest's start, a star shot across the sky a very small distance.

For a moment the three simply stared at the now-black spot in the sky where the shooting star had appeared.

With a modest clearing of his throat, the priest said, "I'll bet Father Christen couldn't have done that."

COLLEEN KEPT A CLOSE EYE on the children, who were carrying trays of cookies from table to table while Maureen, Cassandra and several other women on the events committee poured coffee and tea.

The children wore their jeans and white shirts under green vests that one of the mothers had made, along with derby hats with a buckle on the band. They did their jobs conscientiously and with a style that earned them a lot of attention and even a few tips. Bugsy had run into the kitchen excitedly to report the tips, then, remembering he and Bill were mad at her, turned around and went back to his duties.

Colleen knew Father Gallagher had had a pep talk with the kids before the guests began arriving, urging them to use good manners.

"It'd be easier," Bill had said, "if we weren't wearing these silly clothes."

The priest pretended to look horrified. "Leprechauns are not silly!" he'd insisted, and was explaining the lore to the children when Colleen had been called away to the kitchen. She was happy to see that Bill now wore his costume with confidence and smiled politely as he went from table to table.

Then she caught sight of Claudie, engaged in conversation with a group of older ladies who seemed impressed with her.

She was a smart and beautiful child, and Colleen couldn't imagine how her mother could willingly give up custody of her and Angel to follow a man. Although, now that Colleen was in love with Mike and knew she was losing him, she understood the pain of giving up a man you loved. But she'd never leave her children in order to follow anyone.

Confident that the children were doing a good job, she went back to filling the dishwasher. Other women bustled around the kitchen, cleaning pots and pans in the sink, putting things away, taking inventory of cooking supplies. A few of them sat around a small table in a corner, eating leftovers. Colleen had been invited to join them, but she had no appetite.

She filled the dishwasher, got it started, then scraped the last of the dinner plates and stacked them to go in next.

She tried very hard not to think. She felt sick, though not in the usual way with nausea or fever. Her heart was pounding and her ears rang, as though something in her body clamored to get out.

Her eyes filled with tears and her throat tightened at the realization that what was struggling to escape her was the admission that she'd been wrong yesterday. She'd been trying for hours to figure out what she'd been thinking at the time, but couldn't. How had she interpreted Mike's kindness as some kind of cruelty?

Self-sufficiency was all well and good, to paraphrase Cassandra, but it did not allow for love. She found herself wondering when the ability to cope on her own had become a kind of religion for which she wanted to be martyred. How had dismissing well-meant help become a code to live by rather than accepting it as a kindness to be appreciated?

She didn't know. Couldn't remember. Didn't care. All she understood was that now that she'd thought it through and let those defenses fall, she felt naked and vulnerable. And still very much alone.

She wanted Mike!

But she'd been awful to him. And she could still recall his grimly spoken "Good thing we didn't book a church." In fact, he'd given up rather easily for a man who'd been so determined to get her attention.

Every man, she was sure, had limits when it came to what he'd take from a woman, and she'd apparently surpassed his.

She had to apologize, she thought, even if she couldn't make him understand. But he was working just beyond the kitchen and had been very careful not to look in her direction for fear of catching her eye.

It was entirely possible she wouldn't be able to speak to Mike again before they went their separate ways. She felt panicky and desperate.

"Okay," she told herself, trying to force an inner calm. "Think! You can make him understand. He's always so willing."

MOST OF THE GUESTS had gone except for a few die-hards, Tom and Cassandra included, who continued to dance as the clock struck midnight. The children, whom Mike had expected to have given up in exhaustion long ago, were still high on the evening's excitement. Father Gallagher gave each of them a rosary and a large candy bar for their efforts, and they seemed duly appreciative of both.

Mike walked the edges of the room, folding up chairs, while Clint worked the other side. As he went, he plotted what to do about Colleen. Applying Father Gallagher's theory about using his head rather than his heart, he thought that tying up Colleen, putting her in the van and taking her and the boys home with him was looking better all the time.

His attention was snagged by Claudie and Angel and Bill and Bugsy in urgent conversation. Claudie was pointing to the kitchen as Bill glanced in Mike's direction, then looked away quickly when Mike caught his eye.

They were going to ask him if they could play outside in the dark parking lot—he was sure of it. They'd been paragons of decorum all evening and had to be bursting to let off steam. They'd probably asked Colleen and been refused. He was their last resort.

He hated to turn them down, but he'd have to console them with some alternative entertainment.

When the boys went into the kitchen and the girls came toward him, hand in hand, still wearing their costumes, he began to wonder about his theory. He scooped up three folded chairs in each arm.

"Did you know that leprechauns make shoes?" Claudie asked as she and Angel followed him to the long rolling rack nearby that held the chairs.

"Ah…yes, I think I've heard that." He stacked the chairs on the rack. "When they were hiding, people found them because they heard them hammering."

Angel looked confused. "I didn't know you made shoes with a hammer."

Claudie rolled her eyes. "It's a little hammer with tiny nails. But it still makes a noise."

Angel accepted that. "And leprechauns have gold!" she said excitedly.

"Really. Do you have some?" Mike asked. He began to push the long, unwieldy rack toward the hallway and the storage room. The girls skipped along beside him.

"It's supposed to be in a pot," Angel said, grinning from ear to ear, "only that's not where we keep ours."

The rack in place, Mike turned in time to see Claudie shush Angel in her big-sister way. Angel folded her arms and pouted.

He leaned down to kiss her forehead. "Where do you keep your gold?" he asked.

Before Angel could reply, Claudie put in quickly, "We're supposed to keep the gold a secret. Only, if somebody threatens us, then we have to tell."

"Threaten you with what?"

"I don't know."

"Well. I don't want to be the kind of dad who threatens." He shooed them out the door, then left it open for Clint, who'd be along soon with the other rack.

Claudie and Angel looked at each other worriedly.

"Um…but we want you to know where our treasure is," Claudie insisted.

"Yeah," Angel said, taking his hand, "It's in the—"

Claudie put a hand over Angel's mouth and growled, "Not yet!"

Angel gasped indignantly. "Well, when?"

There was some undercurrent to all this that Mike just wasn't getting.

Looking completely exasperated, Claudie took his wrist and pulled him along with her. "Oh, come on, Daddy. I want you to see the treasure."

"I thought I had to threaten you."

"If I'm a leprechaun for tonight," she said, "I can make my own rules."

He had to give his daughter credit—Claudie was such a clear thinker.

If he could only say the same for Colleen.

EVERYONE ELSE IN THE KITCHEN had left and Maureen and the chairman of the event were getting their coats out of the cloakroom while Colleen gave the counters one last swipe of the dishcloth.

Bill and Bugsy appeared beside her, Bill leaning

his elbow on the counter. They still wore their vests and hats. "Did you know I was magic?" Bill asked with a grin.

She patted his cheek as she ran the cloth under the faucet, then opened it out to dry on the edge of the sink. "Of course. I've always known that about you."

"No, I mean that I can do magic. 'Cause I'm a leprechaun."

"Really." She folded her arms and leaned against the sink. "What can you do? Get a rabbit out of a hat? Find a quarter behind my ear?"

He made a scornful sound. "That's kid stuff."

"You're a kid."

"I'm a leprechaun."

"You're not going to make me disappear, are you?"

He shook his head. "No. But I can make treasure appear."

"Treasure? You mean like buried pirate stuff?"

He stopped to think. "Well, I don't think that's where it came from, but it's treasure."

She looked around. "But I don't see it."

He took her hand. "You have to come with me."

"Okay." If there was a man she'd follow anywhere, it was Bill.

"Lights are going out!" Father Gallagher called.

"Father, wait, we're still…" Colleen shouted as they walked from the kitchen into the main room, but the entire area fell into complete blackness at the loud click of a switch.

Bill held tightly to her hand. "It's okay, Mom," he said. "You'll still be able to see the treasure."

"Okay. I'm with you," she said, hoping Maureen hadn't taken off without them, assuming they'd gone home with the men.

She followed Bill for a dozen steps or so, then he stopped and dropped her hand.

"Is it here?" she asked.

There was no answer. "Bill?" She swung both arms, reaching for Bill or Bugsy.

Instead she connected with a wall of wool. She patted it exploratively and knew instantly that it was not a wall at all, but a man's chest.

The lights went on again, harshly bright, and she found herself looking into Mike Flynn's dusk-blue eyes. They were filled with a love and longing for her that she was surprised and ecstatic to see there, in view of the idiot she'd been about the car door.

"Are you the girls' treasure?" he asked.

"I...I don't know. Bill told me he was taking me to see his treasure...and here *you* are." Colleen's eyes brimmed. "I'm sorry about the car," she whispered, everything inside her beginning to tremble. Was it possible her luck really was changing?

He tipped his head. "I'm sorry I did it without telling you. I thought..."

"No, no," she interrupted. "It was kind. I was just being...hysterically self-protective."

"Then...you'll marry me?"

She was so shocked the proposal still held that she

couldn't speak. As she groped for words that refused to come, she realized that they were being watched. The children were grouped in a nervous little knot, Father Gallagher behind them, and Clint, Maureen, Tom and Cassandra stood to one side, watching shamelessly and waiting for her answer.

"OKAY, THAT'S IT," Mike said as she hesitated, deciding it was time he took control of this situation. It had gotten him in trouble the last time, but he'd be damned if he wasn't going to make the most of this brilliant effort on the children's part. He took Colleen by the hand and strode for the door, pulling her along behind him. He went out the side door of the hall and around to the front, where her scroll was still tacked to the door. He heard footsteps following them.

A small floodlight over the door lit the path from the church hall to the rectory and, happily for him, Colleen's scroll.

"Read that!" he ordered. "You wrote it, and you don't even seem to understand what it's all about."

"But, Mike…"

"Read it."

She focused on the message. "'Peace to all…'" she began.

"Not that part," he interrupted. "Just the last two lines."

She swallowed. "'May love be yours from morn to eve,'" she read, "'and guide you in all you do.'"

"How can you wish that for someone," he asked,

exasperated beyond measure, "and not recognize it when it's offered to you? I love you! I don't want to take you over, push you around, tell you what to do or assume all your challenges. I just want to love you, and for me that involves helping you, supporting you, giving you everything I can give you. But if you hate that and want me to just…"

She put a hand over his mouth. He heard muffled children's laughter somewhere behind them.

"I want you to love me," she said softly, her magic eyes fixed on him with the message of her love. He had to keep staring to make sure he wasn't imagining it. "I think I was afraid of loving you for all you can give me, but that's not it. When I realized I might have to live without you, it wasn't the loss of all the things you can provide that made the future seem so bleak. It was just that *you* wouldn't be there.

"I accept you as my treasure," she said, putting her arms around his neck, "if you'll accept me. I wanted to say that inside, but I couldn't believe you'd be willing to forgive me. Yes, I'll marry you, yes, I'll love you, if you'll love me, and I'll love your children if you'll love mine."

He wrapped her in his arms and their children and friends emerged from the shadows, cheering and applauding.

"I knew it'd work!" Bill said, reaching up for his mother's hug. "When Father Gallagher told us about leprechauns having to tell where the treasure is when somebody threatens to hurt them, Claudie said, 'Your mom and my dad hurt us by not getting together, but we don't even have a treasure to give up.' Then I thought, 'Yes, we do!' And I got the idea about this!''

He turned to Mike, who ruffled his hair and held him close for a moment.

''He's pretty smart,'' Claudie praised. ''I guess if we have to have boys in the family, they're okay.''

Colleen slipped her arms around the little girl and hugged tightly. Then she reached for Bill with her other arm, while Mike got down on one knee to embrace the younger children.

''So, we're really going to do it?'' Bill asked, as though he had to hear the words again. ''You're getting married and we're all going to live with Mike and the girls?''

Everyone waited for Colleen's confirmation. She was a little surprised at the rush of joy she felt when she said unequivocally, ''Yes, we are!''

Mike stood and wrapped his arms around Colleen and held her close, a little stunned that she finally saw things his way. Then, still holding her in one arm, he gathered all the children around them.

''So, we're moving to Boston?'' Bugsy asked.

''I've been thinking about this,'' Mike said, sensing a need for quick action. He wanted details in place before Colleen could change her mind. ''So that the kids only have to change schools once, why don't we look for a house in Cooper's Corner?''

Colleen's eyes widened and she uttered a little sound of disbelief. ''Are you serious?''

"Why not? We all love it here, don't we?" He looked to the children for confirmation and was treated to cheers. The adults who formed their audience looked at one another in smiling surprise.

"But your practice..." Colleen pointed out.

"I'll need about a month or two to close it up and move my office here, sell the condo..."

"But you love the city!" she argued. "You said..."

"I love *you* more," he insisted. "If you'll marry me, I'll live wherever you want to live."

She opened her mouth to offer another protest, but Bill cut her off with a tug on her arm. "Mo-om! He wants to live here! Let's do it!"

"Yeah!" The girls jumped up and down. "Cooper's Corner! Cooper's Corner! Cooper's—"

"You could get married right here!" Maureen put in quickly.

"And I'll prepare the best buffet you've ever tasted," Clint added.

The priest smiled. "Allowing a little time for house hunting and your getting settled," he said, "I can be available the first Saturday in May."

Mike looked into Colleen's eyes. "How about it?"

Her eyes were filled with love for him. It made him feel weak with gratitude. "Let's do it," she said, and threw her arms around him to kiss him again.

"Talk about your pot of gold," he whispered into her ear.

EPILOGUE

Maureen stood in the middle of Twin Oaks' kitchen and couldn't believe the midmorning quiet. Or the fact that she was alone for the first time in…well, she couldn't remember how long it had been.

All their guests had left right after breakfast, and the only couple booked for tonight wouldn't arrive until the middle of the afternoon. Keegan was back in school now that spring break was over, Clint was at the library, and he'd dropped Randi and Robin off to play at a friend's house.

It didn't occur to her to go shopping or luxuriate in a bubble bath. Instead, her mind reeled with the number of tasks she could tackle. Her top priority was the missing boards on the old well behind the house. They'd been in place so long as a protection for children and pets that the long winter had splintered the boards and the rusty old nails had given way. She'd noticed it this morning when she'd been checking to make sure her plants had survived the most recent storm.

Pulling on her jacket and work gloves, she went to

Clint's shop for boards, nails and a hammer, and headed for the well. It was a gorgeous sunny day, if still cold. As she took a deep breath of the pure air, she thought this was one of the bonuses of having to leave New York.

And that was as far as she let the thought go. It was too beautiful a day for stirring up bad memories.

She knelt on the cold, hard earth, put down the boards and hammer and patted her pocket for the nails.

She was just putting the board in place when she heard the softest sigh of sound, and knew instinctively that it had not been made by a foraging deer or raccoon.

Gooseflesh broke out on her scalp and the hair rose along the back of her neck. Long-remembered training slowed just enough by healthy fear made her hesitate a fraction of a second before turning around. That slight delay prevented her from seeing who or what delivered the painful, burning blow to the back of her head.

The last thing she remembered was the headlong rush into moist, cold blackness and the rich smell of the earth as she fell.

When she awoke she was chilled from lying on the damp earth and her head ached. She sat up in panic as she recalled what had happened. Then she glanced up to see daylight and remembered that her great-uncle had filled the well with dirt. She'd fallen only twelve or fourteen feet.

With effort she stood up gingerly, flexing cold, stiff muscles, and searched the dark interior for a hand-hold. There was nothing.

She wondered how long she'd been unconscious and if Clint would miss her when he came home—though that could be hours.

Berating herself for leaving the cell phone in the house, she considered whether she should try climbing up the side of the well or simply preserve her energy and wait for help.

Always a woman of action, she was about to attempt scrabbling up the wall when she heard the dyspeptic sounds of Ed Taylor's truck.

The chickens! He was delivering chickens this morning!

She waited for the truck to stop, the sound of the closing door, then she shouted with all her might, over and over, "Ed! Ed Taylor! Ed, it's Maureen! Ed!"

She stopped. All she heard was silence.

"Ed!" she started again. "Ed Taylor! Ed! Ed!"

Finally a reply sounded in the distance. "Where the heck are you?"

"In the well!" She shuddered with the cold. "In the old well, Ed!"

A couple of minutes later she could see his face and shoulders in the opening. "What are you doing in there?"

"Someone pushed me!" she shouted up. "Can you get me out?"

"I'll be right back," he promised convincingly. "Sit tight, Maureen."

She did. Tight and cold. She wasn't sure if the chill running through her was due to the temperature in the well or her suspicions about who had pushed her.

An image of that day in the New York courtroom filled Maureen's mind. She and her partner, Dan, both detectives with the NYPD, had worked hard to bring Carl Nevil to justice, and the murderer had finally been sent to prison for life.

But Carl reminded Maureen that his brother Owen had been paroled, and there was nothing he'd like better than to get revenge against the cops who'd sent Carl to jail.

That was one of the reasons Maureen had come to Cooper's Corner with Clint. Turning Twin Oaks—the house they'd inherited from their great-uncle Warren Cooper—into a bed-and-breakfast had offered Maureen the chance to ensure the safety of her twin daughters.

But too many unsettling events had occurred in the last few months, from the shooting of one of her guests to an "accident" in the wood shed involving Maureen herself. And when a young woman suffering an overdose had turned up in one of the rooms at Twin Oaks, saying she'd been picked up hitchhiking by a man named Owen Nevil, Maureen knew for certain that her sanctuary had been breached.

Nevil was playing games with her, making sure she

knew he had found her. He was obviously biding his time, since he'd had ample opportunity to harm her.

She would have to be more vigilant now, especially when it came to the twins. Reluctantly, she realized she would have to start keeping her gun close at hand once again. She had no choice. But she vowed she wouldn't live her life in fear.

It was fifteen or twenty minutes later when a thick rope with a type of leather harness was lowered into the well.

"Wrap that around you, Maureen!" The instructions came from a younger voice than Ed's. "Then tighten the buckle."

She thought she recognized the voice. "Alex, is that you?"

Alex McAlester was a veterinarian and Ed's neighbor on the other side.

"Yeah! If you wanted me to come over," he teased, "you could have just invited me for coffee."

"Ha, ha. You rescue animals with this?"

"Yes. And damsels in distress, apparently. You ready?"

"Yes."

"You tighten the buckle?"

"Yes."

"Okay. Turn the winch, Ed."

Maureen heard a grinding sound, then began to make a slow but steady ascent to daylight.

Alex, who had to be six foot six at least, grabbed

Maureen by the arms and hauled her the last few feet out of the hole.

She held on to him gratefully for a moment, then he helped her out of the harness.

Ed came running. She hugged both of them. "Thank God the two of you were around," she said, beginning to shiver. "It was cold in there."

A car door slammed and Clint came running toward them.

"What happened?" he demanded, looking from her to their neighbors to the winch. Then he seemed to answer his own question with the look of big-brother condescension she remembered from their childhood. "Don't tell me you fell into the well."

"I won't," she replied, completely offended. "I'll tell you I was pushed."

The condescending look disappeared, replaced by an expression of mingled anger and alarm. Maureen knew exactly what her brother was thinking.

Owen Nevil.

*   *   *   *   *

*Welcome to Twin Oaks—the new B and B
in Cooper's Corner. Some come for
pleasure, others for passion—
And one to set things straight….*

COOPER'S CORNER

continues with

CRADLE AND ALL
by M. J. Rodgers

When Tom Christen, the new preacher in Cooper's
Corner, found a baby on his doorstep, he wasn't about
to give the infant to some bureaucrat. And Judge
Anne Vandree may have had hair like a halo—but
she was definitely a bureaucrat, informing him that
by law he must surrender the baby. So Tom told her
the truth. He was the baby's father!

Here's a preview!

CHAPTER ONE

"IF YOU HAVE A POINT to make, make it," Tom said.

"The point is," Bender said, taking a step toward Tom, "that's the Kendralls' baby you've got."

Anne noticed a perceptible change in Tom's stance. His legs were slightly spread, as though he was braced for something. Despite the considerable difference in their heights, he looked the burly private investigator straight in the eye.

"This is not the Kendralls' baby," Tom said. "This is my baby."

"You're a priest," Shrubber said, coming to his feet in righteous indignation. "Priests can't have kids."

"He's an Episcopal priest, Mr. Shrubber," Bender said, as if embarrassed to have to explain this fact to his boss. "They're allowed to marry and have kids. They're sort of like Roman Catholic light."

"He didn't have that kid," Shrubber said, his temper showing. "Lindy Olson left that baby with you, Christen, when she found out Bender was closing in. I know it and you know it. Now I'm taking him back to where he belongs."

Tommy's fussing rose to a full-fledged cry at the angry voices.

"You're not taking my baby anywhere," Tom said, his quiet words accelerating like strokes of a piston gathering speed. "Now, get out of here."

For a very long moment, the men stayed exactly where they were, staring at Tom.

"We can do this the easy way, Priest," Shrubber said, taking a small step toward Tom. "Or we can do it the hard way."

Anne was suddenly very afraid. The tension in the room was palpable. She fully expected these men to pounce on Tom at any second and forcibly take the now-screaming baby from him. And she had no doubt, looking at the calm, determined expression on Tom's face, that he would resist them.

She didn't know what to believe about Tommy. She didn't know what to believe about Lindy. She didn't know what to believe about these two men. Only one thing emerged crystal clear in Anne's mind at that moment.

She believed in Tom.

If he said the baby was his, the baby had to be his.

Anne boldly stepped into the room. "You were just told to leave," she roared in a tone that had quelled many a courtroom.

Shrubber and Bender whirled around to face her.

"And who in the hell are you?" Shrubber demanded.

"Anne Vandree, associate justice of the Berkshire Court."

Shrubber's eyes took in Anne's petite frame as though he were sizing up her mettle. The guy didn't know the first thing about mettle. Something that was probably meant to be a smile, but emerged much more as a sneer, drew back his lips.

"Why should I believe you are who you say?" Shrubber demanded more than asked.

Anne sent the attorney a lethal look, the kind she only reserved for his particular brand of scum. Her voice descended into its deadliest delivery. "I don't have to prove anything to you. The state police are on their way. They know me. It's your credentials they'll be checking when they arrest you for trespassing."

Bender's eyes shot nervously toward Shrubber. Anne knew that he was looking to his boss for his next instructions.

Shrubber blinked, a quick reassessment of both Anne and the situation flashing through his squinting eyes.

Anne took another step toward him. "I don't know what the judges are like where you come from, but here in the Berkshires we throw the book at outsiders who barge into private homes making threats."

"We didn't barge in," Bender said, his squeaky voice clearly on the defensive. "Father Christen let us in."

"I just heard him tell you to get out," Anne said.

"I don't think you understand the gravity of this matter," Shrubber said, his tone suddenly far more conciliatory. "If the state police do arrive, the matter will be taken out of my hands and I'll have to file official charges."

"I'd be interested to know how you can file charges against a man for refusing to hand over his child," Anne said, boldly advancing another step.

"That is not his child," Shrubber said.

"Oh, yes it is," Anne replied, marching over to stand beside Tom, not taking her eyes off Shrubber for a second.

"And just how do you know that?" Shrubber demanded.

Anne took the screaming baby out of Tom's arms and hugged him to her. Tommy clung to her as she gently hushed his anguished sounds.

"Because I'm the baby's mother," Anne announced with a fierceness that shocked even her.